MISFIT LOVE 2

THE FINALE

JADE JONES

WEBSITE

www.jadedpublications.com

TEXT BOOKS TO 55444

Join the Jaded fam to
be the first to hear about new releases, contests,
and giveaways!

MOVIES STREAMING ON TUBI

"FANATIC" is now streaming on Tubi

"CAMERON" is now streaming on Tubi

OTHER TITLES BY THIS AUTHOR

When a Gangsta Wants You

BOSS

Captivated by a Savage

Haunted Love

ABOUT THE AUTHOR

Jade Jones discovered her passion for creative writing in elementary school. Born in 1989, she began writing short stories and poetry as an outlet. Later on, as a teen, she led a troubled life which later resulted in her becoming a ward of the court. Jade fell in love with the art and used storytelling as a means of venting during her tumultuous times.

Aging out of the system two years later, she was thrust into the dismal world of homelessness. Desperate, and with limited income, Jade began dancing full time at the tender age of eighteen. It wasn't until Fall of 2008 when she finally caught her break after being accepted into Cleveland State University. There, she lived on campus and majored in Film and Television. Now, six years later, she flourishes from her childhood dream of becoming a bestselling author. Since then, she has written the best-selling "Cameron" series. She also writes women's fiction under the pen name Pebbles Starr.

Quite suitably, she uses her life's experiences to create captivating characters and story lines. Jade currently resides in Atlanta, Georgia. With no children, she spends her leisure shopping and traveling. She says that seeing new faces, meeting new people, and experiencing diverse cultures fuels her creativity. The stories are generated in her heart, the craft is practiced in her mind, and she expresses her passion through ink.

SYNOPSIS

Sky, Rebel, and the crew are back in the explosive final installment of *Misfit Love*. With her heart pulled in three directions, Sky finds herself navigating a dangerous love triangle: her loyal childhood friend Rebel, who's always had her back; her toxic baby daddy, who refuses to let go; and a ruthless Armenian kingpin with an agenda of his own.

But love isn't Sky's only battle. Tensions boil over when her friendship with Zuri takes a sharp turn, and their bond is tested over a new love interest. As betrayal, jealousy, and secrets threaten to unravel everything, Sky must decide who to trust and where her loyalties truly lie.

Will love conquer all, or will the weight of lies and revenge shatter their worlds forever? Get ready for one last, unforgettable ride packed with heart-pounding twists and raw emotion!

1

REBEL

"**R**eb," Halee murmured, her voice low and sweet, "come back to bed." She'd been watching me stare out of our bedroom window at the LA skyline for the past hour, pining after Sky.

Like a slave forced to servitude, I did as she asked. Halee pulled the sheets over us, then slid closer to me, her hand brushing against my chest. I could tell she wanted some dick. The dim glow of the city lights outside spilled through the windows, casting soft shadows on the room.

I wasn't in the mood, so I pulled away, sitting up on the edge of the mattress. "Not tonight, Halee," I muttered.

Her hand froze mid-reach, and I felt her shift behind me. "What's wrong? You've been distant all week."

I looked out of the window again, wishing I could escape from this fucked up reality, the Los Angeles skyline sprawling in the distance. What could I say? That Sky was all I thought about? That every time I closed my eyes, I saw her face?

"It's just... work," I said, running a hand through my locs.

Halee's voice hardened. "This isn't about work. It's about her, isn't it?"

My shoulders tensed. She didn't have to say Sky's name; we both knew who she was talking about.

I stood up, grabbing my hoodie off the chair. "I need some air."

"Don't walk away from me!" Halee's voice sharpened, frustration spilling out. "Rebel, we need to talk. You've been checked out for days, and I'm trying to fix this."

I paused, my back to her, the weight of her words pressing against me. Fix this? How the hell could she fix something that was broken from the jump?

"I'm not in the mood for this, Halee," I said, pulling the hoodie over my head. "I've got shit on my mind."

Her voice softened, almost pleading. "I'm your wife, Reb. I just want us to be okay."

I turned toward the window, my reflection staring back at me in the glass. Sky's face flashed in my mind—the way she smiled, the way she looked at me like I was everything. And now, I'd made it so I'd never see that look again.

"We're fine," I said, the lie hanging heavy in the air as I turned toward the window, staring out at the dark cityscape.

Too bad me and Sky weren't fine—not even close. I didn't wanna cause her anger. I didn't wanna cause her pain. I didn't wanna cause her grief. The only reason I had come back into Sky's life was to make her happy—and I couldn't do that as long as my circumstances remained the same.

It was childish and selfish to expect Sky to wait for me to get my shit together. The truth was, I would never be able to get out of this marriage as long as my family was indebted to Tommie. I was in this shit till death do us part—and not even my love for Sky could change that, so I accepted it for what it was.

But even as I told myself to let her go, my mind betrayed me, wandering back to the times we'd shared in adulthood and childhood. I found myself wondering what she was up to. Every day I fought the urge to call her or surprise her with dinner and lavish gifts. I wanted to do everything in my power to get her to forgive me. But the best thing I could do for her was to leave her alone. I couldn't stand the thought of causing her any more pain.

"I love you, Rebel," Halee purred, sliding up behind me and wrapping her arms around my waist. Her voice yanked me out of my thoughts, but my heart was still with Sky.

I tensed, not wanting to let her in. "Yeah?" I muttered.

She kissed my shoulder and leaned her chin against my back. "And I've got good news," she whispered.

"What's that?" I asked, unenthused, my voice flat. I really didn't care what she had to say. All I cared about was Sky.

"You aren't gonna believe this," she said, her voice trembling with excitement. "But after five years of trying endlessly... I'm finally pregnant," she beamed. "We're gonna have a baby!"

Before I could respond, I heard gunshots coming from our guesthouse, where my father and step-mom lived.

Pushing Halee away, I rushed out of the room in nothing but my briefs and hoodie. I was so determined to check on my parents, I forgot to grab my gun for protection.

"Rebel?! REBEL!" Halee screamed after me.

"Stay here!" I told her on my way out.

Racing out of the mansion at breakneck speed, I sprinted to the guesthouse barefoot and found their door wide open.

POP!

POP!

Two more gunshots cracked through the air, and when I burst into the living room, the scene stopped me cold. Blood was everywhere—on the walls, the furniture, pooling on the floor. My father's body was crumpled on the carpet, his face unrecognizable from two close-range shots. My stepmom was still breathing, but just barely, clutching at her chest where two bullets had torn through her back.

And there stood Tommie, calm as ever, holding a smoking automatic like it was just another day at the office. His smug-ass grin set my blood on fire.

"YOU SICK FUCK!" I bellowed, the rage inside me exploding. Without thinking, I charged at him like a wild animal. "MUTHAFUCKA, I'MMA KILL YOU!"

POP!

Tommy shot me in the leg at point blank range, halting me dead in my tracks.

WHAM!

Before I could register the pain of being shot, Flex appeared out of nowhere and punched me in the face. With all that was going on, I didn't even see him enter the room. Tommie had two more of his henchmen with him, just in case he couldn't handle me on his own.

Pussy nigga.

I fell to the floor, nose dislocated, and heart broken in two. If only I'd gotten here sooner. I might've been able to save them.

"I been waitin' on this shit," Flex said before kicking me in the face.

Blood sprayed onto the wall as he assaulted me. Halee burst into the room, her screams piercing the air as she caught sight of her in-laws' lifeless bodies sprawled across the floor. Tears streamed down her face as she dropped to her knees, wailing hysterically.

Tommie's men wasted no time grabbing her. "Get her outta here," he barked, his voice cold and steady. They dragged her away, kicking and screaming, ignoring her cries as she tried to break free.

"Daddy, no! NO, DADDY! Don't kill him!" Halee's voice

cracked, desperation pouring out with every word. "Please, don't kill him, Daddy! Please! I'm pregnant!"

Her words hung heavy in the air as the door slammed shut behind her, leaving me alone with the devil himself.

"I don't give a fuck," Tommie said once she was out of earshot. "I'll just find some other sucker from South Central. He'll help raise the lil' bastard."

"Tommie...why?" I struggled to ask through puffy lips and a broken nose, my voice barely above a whisper.

Tommie crouched in front of me, his eyes cold as ice. Wordlessly, he pulled out his phone, opened his photos app, and shoved the screen in my face. My stomach churned at the three grisly images staring back at me.

The first was the mangled body of the nigga who'd tried to rob me in El Paso. I thought I'd killed his ass, but there he was. Plain as day. He must've somehow gotten away before Tommie finally caught up to him. The second photo was his girl, lifeless and mutilated. But the third... The third made me freeze. It was a butchered baby girl. Her tiny body, torn and bloodied, was something I'd never be able to unsee.

Hell, even I wouldn't have gone that far.

"You were supposed to be my enforcer," Tommie said, ignoring my shock. His voice was calm, but his rage simmered beneath the surface. "But what good is an enforcer that doesn't enforce?" His tone turned sharp, venomous. "I had to track that muthafucka down myself and finish the job! You know I hate getting my hands dirty! That's what I have you assholes for!" He kicked me hard in the ribs, sending a fresh wave of pain through my battered body.

"Then, on top of that," he continued, voice rising, "I find out you've been stealing from me!" His face twisted with fury, but I caught the glint of betrayal in his tear-filled eyes. "I trusted you, Rebel. You were my son," he said, his voice cracking with emotion.

"I'm...still your son," I croaked, the words coming out slow and weak.

Tommie shook his head. "No," he said. "You're a wolf in sheep's clothing."

I tried to grab his leg but he stepped out of my reach.

"I trusted you," he repeated. "I brought you into my circle, into my business, into my family." He shook his head. "I only let your parents live for as long as they did out of the respect I had for you. But since you lost all my respect, there's no reason why they should continue to waste oxygen."

POP!

He shot my step-mom in the back one last time, halting all movement. He wanted to hurt me just as bad as I'd hurt him. And the only way to truly hurt me was by hurting them.

Suddenly, I hated myself for treating them like a burden. Sure, they were flawed. But at the end of the day, they were still family.

Tommie handed Flex his gun. "Handle this shit for me. I'm done wasting time on this prick."

"With pleasure," Flex smiled before putting six rounds in me.

POP!

POP!

POP!

POP!

POP!

POP!

After leaving me in a puddle of my own blood, they slipped out of the guesthouse as quietly as they'd arrived. Halee's sobs had faded, and I couldn't tell if they'd taken her with them or left her behind. My body screamed in pain, every nerve on fire, but through blurred vision, I caught sight of my stepmom. Her fingers twitched faintly. She was still alive—hanging on by a thread.

Using what little strength I had left, I dragged myself toward her, each inch feeling like a mile. When I finally reached her, I covered her trembling hand with mine. A single tear streaked down my face, hot and bitter. Before I could process the reality of it all—the death, the betrayal, the chaos—I blacked out, swallowed by the darkness.

2

FLEX

I walked out of Rebel's Hollywood Hills home, feeling like the muthafuckin' man. I'd been patiently waiting to get my lick-back after the way that nigga bitched me in the club. Tonight, justice was finally served on a silver platter and I had never felt more righteous. My ass was on cloud nine until Tommie suddenly snatched me up outside.

"Don't think I won't deal your ass the same hand! If you think I'mma let that bitch get away with stealing from me, then you're sadly fuckin' mistaken, friend! I got a hollow point with her name on it! And one for you too if I find out you were in on it!"

"I—I had no idea my girl was stealing from you, Boss!" I lied. "Zuri don't really talk to me about work. I ain't got shit to do with her schemes. On my granny! I ain't like that, Boss. You can trust me."

"Then prove it," he said.

I knew exactly what he was getting at. I heard him loud and clear. He wanted to me to handle Zuri like I'd handled Rebel.

"You got it," I promised. "I'll handle it."

"You'd better. 'Cuz if you don't handle that bitch, I'mma handle you."

As I climbed into the back of Tommie's Escalade, I got a text message from my nigga, Melvin, who used to do security with me at the club in Culver City. His text was accompanied with a photo of me and Fatima laid up in bed naked. His message said:

Really my nigga??? This the shit you into????

"What the fuck?" I muttered under my breath.

The jig was finally up! My skeletons were tumbling out of the closet, and it took everything in me not to turn the gun on my damn self.

Now, instead of burying one bitch, I had to dig two graves.

3

SKY

Haven and I had been laid up together for two whole days. Despite sharing a bed, we hadn't crossed any lines, and I was grateful he didn't push the issue. My heart just wasn't in it. The sting of Zuri and Rebel's betrayals was still fresh, cutting deeper than I cared to admit.

The way I saw it, it was better to have an enemy slap you in the face than a friend stab you in the back. At least you could see the enemy coming.

Tommie hadn't threatened to press charges, and for that, I was thankful. It was the only silver lining in a storm cloud that refused to pass. I still hadn't heard from Rebel, and I couldn't say I was surprised. His disappearing act was nothing new. He'd warned me about his inconsistency, but knowing it didn't make it hurt any less.

Since I woke up before Haven and Chosen, I decided to cook breakfast. I washed my hands, pulled out the pots and pans, and tried to focus on the mundane task. But just as I set the skillet on the stove, Chosen shuffled into the kitchen, rubbing his sleepy eyes.

Mommy, when can I play my game with Rebel? he signed.

The mention of Rebel's name hit me like a punch to the gut. My throat tightened, and before I could stop it, tears blurred my vision. I didn't even know why it hurt so much. Maybe it was the hope Chosen still had in Rebel, or maybe it was the realization that part of me did too.

Closing the cabinet, I kneeled in front of him and pulled him towards me. "Baby... listen to me... Rebel is with his family now and you won't be seeing him for a while."

But why? I like Rebel, he signed.

"I like him too but Rebel has his own family," I explained.

He can have two families, Chosen argued.

"No, baby. Your Daddy won't like that," I told him.

"My Daddy?" he asked, confused.

I took a seat at the kitchen table, put my son on my lap, and had a heart-to-heart with him about his real father. For the past two days, Chosen simply thought Haven was a friend. He didn't know he was his dad because Haven had gotten locked up when he was just a baby.

After hearing the truth about Haven, he climbed off my lap, and prepared to leave.

"Would you like to play your game with your dad?" I asked him.

"No!" he pouted. "I wanna play with Rebel!"

I couldn't argue with that, so I watched as he stormed out of the kitchen with an attitude. Rebel had his own family and sooner or later, my son had to come to terms with that.

Haven had his issues, but at least I knew what I was getting with him. Plus, we had history and a child together. Part of me felt obligated to make it work with my baby daddy.

Besides, I needed someone to lean on during these trying times. Someone to protect me. I knew Haven wouldn't let anything happen to us. Speaking of Haven, he walked into the kitchen a couple minutes after his son left and kissed me.

"Good morning," I smiled.

"Mornin', love bug."

"How'd you sleep?" I asked him.

"Great, now that I'm not wakin' up on a cold, hard bunk. What'chu cookin'?"

"Eggs, bacon, and pancakes. Chosen's favorite."

Haven's smile slowly vanished. "Have you told him about me yet?"

"I just did..."

"Oh yeah? How'd he take it?"

"How do you think?" I asked. "He was just a baby when you got locked up. Give him time. Right now, he doesn't understand."

"He doesn't understand 'cuz you done had all these different niggas around him," he said.

I cut my eyes at Haven and he quickly backtracked. "Look, I ain't tryin' to tongue-wrestle with you. I'm tryin' to make this shit work."

"I can see that you're trying," I said in agreement.

"I wanna be honest and upfront with you always. I don't want there to be any secrets or miscommunication between us. So, with that said, there's somethin' I gotta tell you."

"What is it?"

Haven took a deep breath, then told me all about how he married some bitch in prison for visitation rights. He claimed that she smuggled in shit for him to sell to the inmates and that their relationship was strictly business. He also told me that he planned to file for a divorce now that he was home. By the time, he finished I felt like I was experiencing déjà vu.

"I understand you had to do what you had to in order to survive in prison," I said once he was finished. "Now you need to understand that you can't come back here until your ass is divorced."

～

THREE DAYS LATER, I was finally starting to feel like myself again —or so I thought.

"Hey, beautiful..." a deep, sexy voice said from behind me, smooth and steady, like he already knew I'd turn around.

I pivoted slowly, curiosity pulling me despite myself. There he stood—my man, exuding effortless confidence in a crisp, black Puma tracksuit that hugged his athletic frame just right. A diamond tennis chain glimmered against his brown skin, catching the sunlight like it had been placed there specifically to hypnotize me. And damn, if it wasn't working.

"Hey, yourself," I shot back, my voice sharp with sass, but my heart betraying me with its quickened pace.

The warm wind teased at my hair, blowing strands into my face as if the universe was giving me a moment to gather myself. It was one of those hot, dry Los Angeles afternoons where the breeze seemed to play peek-a-boo, showing up just long enough to remind you it was there. The kind of day made for hiking at Runyon or strolling barefoot along the beach, soaking in the perfection of the California sun.

But here I was, staring into the ocean blue eyes of the man I had sworn—on more than one occasion—I'd stop fucking with. His eyes sparkled with a mix of mischief and something softer, something that made me feel as shaky as a Jenga tower on its last block.

"What are you doing here?" I asked, crossing my arms in front of me as a thin shield of protection. Not that it would do much good. He always knew how to find the cracks.

"I'm here 'cuz a nigga got good news," he beamed, grinning from ear to ear.

Whenever he smiled, I just melted. It was my kryptonite, and in that moment, I forgot why I was even mad at his ass. "Oh yeah? And what's that?" I asked, folding my arms tighter across my D cups.

That convenient breeze stopped blowing and my hair fell over my shoulders. I'd recently cut it into an asymmetrical bob.

"Shit's all the way together now," he said with an arrogant smirk.

What's that mean?

Did he take care of the things he needed to take care of?

Did he finally file those divorce papers?

I wasn't easily convinced, and I still had my doubts and reservations about him, so I simply stared at him for several seconds. "Is *that* right?" I asked skeptically.

He slowly walked over to me and gently grabbed my wrist. His touch was so comforting, like coming home after being away for an eternity.

"Damn right. Everything's handled on my end," he said, tugging me towards him. "From here on out, it's just us."

Haven cupped my face and placed a delicate kiss on my forehead. The feel of his skin and the comforting sound of his heartbeat against my chest reminded me just how much I had been missing and longing for him in his absence.

"Me and you against the world." Taking my hands in his, he kissed the back of each one and a warm fuzzy feeling filled me up from the inside out.

"Against the world?" I grinned. "Or against your soon-to-be ex?" I teased.

My son, who stood off in the distance, darted his blue eyes back and forth between us as we shared an intimate moment in the parking lot of my apartment building. I was just leaving out when Haven suddenly showed up out of nowhere. Me and Chosen were on our way to the grocery store.

Until he handled his affairs, I refused to see or even speak to him. The last thing I wanted was more trouble in my life. I'd already made enough of it on my own.

"Against whatever comes our way," he said, leaning in to kiss my lips.

I slid my hands up his chest and wrapped them around his neck. He pulled me into him and I melted against his strong, broad body. Meanwhile, my son stood beside us, rolling his eyes at our public affection. It was still taking some getting used to for him.

"You really drive me crazy," Haven whispered against my lips. "And at the same time, I've never felt so calm and balanced." He kissed me again. "You know I really love your ass, right?" He conveyed his true feelings word for word with an unwavering gaze.

I nodded. Sure, we'd had our ups and downs...and he had made some fucked up choices, but as a bottle girl who stole and scammed for a living, I wasn't exactly a saint either.

"I know I haven't always kept it real wit'chu. I know there was shit I said and did that hurt you in the process...but I want you to know, Sky...shit's gone be different now," he said. "From here on out, I am one hunnid percent *fully* committed and invested in you."

"Only me?"

He kissed my knuckles. "My heart belongs to you and only you, baby," he told me. "I love you, bae..."

Despite our differences, I fell against his chest and whispered, "I love you, too, baby." Something about those heartfelt confessions made me surrender to him without shame. They just got me every time.

We were basking in our glory when a black Challenger suddenly pulled into the parking lot of my apartment. Their loud music immediately grabbed my attention, followed by the sound of their bald tires screeching. They were bumping trap music as they sped towards us erratically, burning rubber in their haste.

Before I could say or do anything, the passenger pointed an automatic out of his window and fired his gun in our direction. I couldn't see who he was because he was wearing a Fendi face mask that hid his identity, but I knew, without a shadow of a doubt, that he was determined to kill us all.

TAT! TAT! TAT! TAT! TAT! TAT! TAT! TAT!

Time seemed to slow as hollow points tore through the air at lightning speed, ripping into the love of my life. Two of the bullets passed through his body, striking my son, who stood directly behind him, in the chest.

I barely had a chance to grab and shield my six-year-old as he and my man crashed to the concrete, bodies riddled with holes.

Instinctively, I got down too—but only because I didn't want to be shot as well.

A bloodcurdling scream rang out and it took me several moments to realize it had come from me. It didn't even sound like my voice; it was like some unfamiliar sound had erupted from inside my chest. The shooting only lasted for a second but it was the longest second of my life.

When I finally looked behind me, I saw that the driver was now making a swift U-turn. Now that he'd done what he came to do, he peeled out of the parking lot faster than the bullets he'd let fly.

"No! No! No! No! No!" I cried, crawling over to my son. "CHOSEN?!" My voice cracked with emotion as I called out to him. "Chosen! Chosen, baby, get up!"

He wasn't moving and it looked like he wasn't breathing either, but I was too afraid to check his pulse to verify it.

Why the hell did I just stand there frozen?

Why didn't I throw my body in front of his?

Why the fuck didn't I do more to protect him?

"Chosen...please, baby...*pleeeaassee*...baby, please...please... Get up for Mommy, baby," I begged, bawling my eyes out.

I glanced at his blood-soaked shirt, then at Haven who was stretched out less than three feet away. He, too, was motionless.

Slowly but surely, neighbors started to pour out of their

homes to see what had happened. They'd all heard the gunshots. As a matter of fact, everyone in a twenty-mile radius had heard them.

This shit is not happening!

This shit is not fucking happening, I told myself over and over again.

I felt like I was trapped in someone else's nightmare.

"This is not happening!" I finally said aloud in a shaky tone.

Was this karma?

Was this revenge?

I had robbed so many niggas, there was really no telling who had come after me. All I knew was that this shit was unreal!

No! No! No!

Chosen, baby, you're going to be okay, I thought to myself in denial. *Mommy's gonna get you some help, baby.*

I wasn't ready to accept losing him. A mother wasn't supposed to bury her child—especially her only child.

"What happened?" a fellow resident in my apartment asked, as if the shit wasn't already obvious.

"Oh my God! THE BABY'S BEEN HIT!!!" another said as they checked my son's pulse. "OH MY GOD!!! Somebody, call 911!"

"CALL 911!" a second person yelled.

Why didn't they kill me too, I asked myself?

Why the fuck didn't they just kill my ass too?

Clenching my son's bloodstained shirt, I pressed my tearstained face against his chest and sobbed wretchedly.

As they continued to murmur in the distance, I slowly looked down at my own clothes and the dark red blood I was covered in.

This shit is all my fault, I told myself. *This shit is all my fucking fault!*

4

BLADE

I had popped that nigga Haven like a Tic Tac! And if I could, I would've recorded the shit just to watch over and over again with a box of popcorn.

Haven should've had his niggas bury my ass the day they jumped me at the bar. Clearly, he had underestimated me. He was too busy shacking up with Sky to remember what goes around comes around. He'd also failed to realize that one of my arms was still operable and I had no problem squeezing a trigger.

When Jessica came back home with the money she'd taken from me, the first thing I did was hit up my niggas in the hood to roll up on Haven's block. I couldn't drive a car *and* bust a hammer myself. So I called in the reinforcements.

"Damn. You gave dat nigga them rounds," my boy Smurf cheered as he steered the Challenger.

I pulled the Fendi mask off my face and smiled as we merged onto the freeway.

"Ain't no comin' back from dat," he said.

"Yeah... But I fucked around and hit the kid too," I sighed. "I ain't mean to do that shit, bro."

"Aye. That lil' nigga should've tucked and rolled when he heard them shots," Smurf laughed.

I didn't see a damn thing funny—especially since Chosen was deaf.

Damn, did I kill him, I wondered.

I didn't intend for the lil' nigga to get hurt. I was aiming at Haven's bitch ass. I didn't anticipate Chosen standing directly behind him. If he died, that blood would be on my hands and my conscience.

Regardless, I had to clap at that nigga Haven. Cousin or no cousin, that nigga had to catch a hot one. If I didn't bury him first, he was gonna bury me last. It was kill or be killed. I had no choice but to make the first move.

Still, I hated that Chosen had gotten caught in the crosshairs of our feud. The thought of it sat heavy in my chest, bringing back memories of my younger brother, taken too soon in a drive-by, just like this one. Life was a vicious cycle, spinning faster than any of us could escape.

"Fuck it," I muttered, more to myself than anyone else. "It is what it is. I told that nigga I wasn't no bitch."

But deep down, I knew better. Karma wasn't done with me yet.

5

SKY

"We've got a gunshot wound victim with internal hemorrhaging," a nurse said as they wheeled Chosen on a stretcher toward the O.R. He wasn't moving, and his breathing was shallow, barely supported by the machines.

I was so consumed with the state of his health, I didn't even notice where they'd taken Haven. My son was my only priority. It was a miracle he was still alive, but his chances of surviving the night were slim—he'd lost so much blood. One of his lungs had been punctured, leaving him struggling to breathe on his own.

"Chosen, baby, Mommy's with you," I said in a shaky tone. "Mommy's with you and you're going to make it, baby. You're strong. You hear me? You're a fighter. So fight for me, baby. Fight for Mommy," I begged.

"Ma'am, you'll need to wait in the waiting room," the nurse said firmly, blocking me as I tried to follow them to the operating room.

"I am not waiting in a fucking waiting room!" I snapped. A waiting room was where I was told my parents had passed away. I'd be damned if I relived that horror. "I'm his mother! I'm gonna be right by his side no matter what! Fuck a waiting room!"

The nurse immediately got irate with me. "Ma'am, you cannot come into the O.R!"

I was about to go in on her ass when a pair of arms grabbed me from behind. At first, I thought it was Rebel, but when I turned around, I saw Zuri standing there, her face soft with sympathy.

On my way to the hospital, I'd sent both of them a text. I'd also reached out to my cousin, Leilani, and even tried calling Rebel, but his phone went straight to voicemail. Thankfully, Zuri came through for me. Leilani hadn't shown up yet, but knowing her, she was probably stuck in LA's rush-hour traffic, fighting her way here.

"Everything's going to be okay, sis! I'm here now," Zuri said in tears. She was an emotional wreck like me and I was surprised to see that Flex wasn't with her.

With everything that had taken place, I needed as much support as I could get—even if it came from my enemies.

The nurses continued on with their journey and I stayed behind to hug Zuri and cry on her shoulder. I didn't care about our fight or the fact that she'd thrown me under the bus in Tommie's office. None of that shit mattered now. I was simply grateful to have someone to lean on. I couldn't go through this shit alone. This shit was too much for one person to handle. Besides, a bitch was still shaken up from all the hysteria. And my ears were still ringing from the gunfire. I was scarred after the shit I'd just experienced.

"Oh, Zuri, it was awful!" I cried. "They shot Chosen, Z! THEY SHOT MY BABY!" I wailed, clenching her shirt close to my tear-soaked face. "Who the fuck shoots a child?!"

"A hoe ass nigga, that's who."

"I can't believe they shot my baby," I sobbed hysterically, body still trembling from the aftershock.

"*Sshh*, it's gonna be okay, sis," she said, rubbing my hair. "Chosen's gonna pull through, as well as Haven. They're both gonna pull through. Just trust me, okay?"

I truly hoped so.

Because if I lost my son, I'd have no reason to go on. Chosen was my heart and soul, an extension of me. My whole world, my everything.

For several minutes, I stood in the hallway of the hospital, holding my former best friend while bawling my eyes out. I was covered in Chosen's blood, visibly shaken and unable to feel anything except fear—and regret for all the fucked up shit I'd done.

I should've never stolen from all those people while working at Club Allure. I should've never gotten involved in that scamming and robbing shit. Now my sins had come back to haunt me. Life was a boomerang and you got what you gave.

I still didn't know who had shot at us, but I would bet money it was someone looking to seek revenge. Maybe even Tommie! That nigga was pissed about us stealing from him!

The sudden realization slapped me in the face.

What if it was Tommie? What if this was his way of punishing me for taking that money and lying about it? After all, he did pull a gun on me and Zuri after finding out we had scammed him. He'd already proven himself to be vindictive, and he had more than enough motive to kill me.

That fat, greasy-haired, Armenian piece of shit!

I'm gonna blow holes into that muthafucka if he did this!

I swear to God, I'm gonna kill his ass!

Snatching away from Zuri, I stormed towards the exit, silent but determined. I was so damn mad, all I saw was red! I didn't even bother to tell her what I had up my sleeve. All I could think about was fucking up that white bastard!

"Sky? Sky?!" Zuri called after me, shirt stained in my baby's blood. "Where the hell are you going?!" she asked, confused by my abruptness.

"To find Tommie!" I yelled over my shoulder.

Zuri quickly caught up with me and grabbed my arm before I could leave. "Sky, you are not thinking clearly!"

"Tommie, he..." I shook my head frantically. "He did this shit, Zuri! He did this shit! I know he did!" I told her plain and simple.

"Sky, Tommie would never—"

"Z, you saw that crazy look in his eyes the day we were in his office!" I argued. "I mean for God's sake, the nigga pulled a gun on us! Don't tell me you took that shit lightly! Because I sure as hell didn't!"

"That doesn't mean he was going to use it! Look, Tommie's a lot of things but he ain't a fucking murderer! Not only that, but do you really think he would've killed us in a crowded club?!"

I continued to shake my head in denial. "Tommie did this!" I insisted.

"Sky...Tommie is not some killer—"

"You don't know that," I told her. "You don't know that shit, Z. When pushed over the edge, a person is capable of doing anything, including murder!"

Zuri shook her head in disagreement.

"Look!" I tossed my hands up in the air. "I don't give a fuck what you say. I saw the way that nigga looked at us that night. He wanted to body our asses for stealing that money from him. What if this..." I paused and swallowed the lump in my throat. "What if this was his way of exacting revenge? What if he sent them niggas to blow at us?"

Zuri gave me a sad, sympathetic look. "Sky...listen to yourself. *Exacting revenge*? Bitch, this is Tommie we're talking about. Not Al fucking Capone! I get that you've just been through a traumatic experience, but let's try to think logically here."

"Bitch, fuck logic! My son is fighting for his fucking life! The only thing I can think about is payback!"

Zuri reached out to comfort me, but I pulled back. I was pissed that she didn't agree with me on this one.

"Sky, please don't go! Chosen needs you!" she cried out as I kept walking. "SKY?!"

Her voice cracked behind me, but I didn't stop. I pushed through the doors, my mind locked on one thing: confronting Tommie on my own.

6

TOMMIE

I was in my office at Club Allure, just hours before opening, going over inventory for the newest establishment my father planned to launch, when the door swung open.

Sky stormed in, looking madder than a muthafucka, her fists clenched and eyes blazing with rage.

Sheesh. Who shit in her cereal, I thought. *And what would possess her to storm into my office like that*? *Who the fuck did this black bitch think she was*?

I was the one who should've been pissed! Her thieving ass had been stealing from me for only God knows how long, then she had the nerve to stand in my face and lie about the shit. Like I wouldn't find out. Her ass had gotten me for over $15,000 in a single month, so there was no telling how much money she'd taken during the span of her employment. Hundreds of thousands of dollars, if I had to guess.

"Sky..." I slowly stood to my feet and clasped my hands together in front of me. "To what do I owe the honor of this unexpected visit?" I asked her. Deep down inside, I was happy to see her but I couldn't tell her that. I most definitely couldn't show it after the way she did me.

Sky walked over to my desk and slapped all the papers on top of it to the floor. "Why the fuck do you think I'm here?!" she yelled. "What? You thought you weren't gon' answer for that shit you pulled?"

Suddenly, two of my security guards stormed in, but I held up a hand signaling them to back down. I could handle Sky's temperamental ass on my own.

"What the fuck are you talkin' about?" I growled, picking up the paperwork once we were alone again.

Sky surprised me when she mushed me in the head. Never in my life had a person done that shit and lived to tell the tale. I almost called my shooters back in to deal with her ass.

"Nigga, you know what the fuck I'm talking about!" she shouted. "You sent them muthafuckas to shoot at me! Because of you, my son is laid up in a fucking hospital, fighting for his life!" Hot tears streamed down her cheeks and I finally understood her rage.

"Sky," I began in a calm tone. "I had no idea—"

"Don't act like you had nothing to do with it! I know you put the hit out on me!"

"Sky, I swear to you, I would never put you or your son's life in danger," I assured her.

Seeing her in the distraught state that she was in made me wanna pull her close to me and just hold her. I wouldn't harm a hair on her head. In spite of the way I treated her, I really did love the fuck out of her ass. I always had and I always would.

"You gotta believe me. I am not responsible for the shit you're accusing me of," I told her in a calm, even-tempered tone.

"Bullshit!" she hollered. "Your ass pulled a gun on me the other day!"

"I was just bluffin'," I said earnestly. "The gun wasn't even loaded."

"You threatened to kill me!" she reminded me.

"Sky..." I placed the paperwork onto my desk and slowly made my way toward her. "The things I said then... I didn't mean none of that shit. I mean, what did you expect from me? I was hurt, angry...disappointed. You had me thinking I could trust you. Led me to believe you were an entirely different person only to switch up on me. I was pissed," I admitted. "But I would never endanger you or your son to prove a point. And I am *incredibly* sorry to hear about what happened to him. If you need anything, Sky...anything at all—"

"The only thing I need from you is the truth," she said with tear-filled eyes. "My baby might not make it to see tomorrow. The least you can do is tell me who pulled the trigger. I know you aren't the type of nigga to get your own hands dirty. So tell me...who did you pay to shoot at me?"

"Sky, I—"

"Don't stand in my face and lie to me any longer than you already have!" she demanded.

"Sky—"

Suddenly, she reached in her purse and pulled out a pistol. Nothing too crazy. Just a small handgun. But despite its size, it was still able to claim a life. "Nigga, you must think I'm playing with your ass." She cocked the hammer.

"Sky, I'm tellin' you now...you'd better put that shit away if you don't plan on using it," I warned her.

Before she could make her move, I snatched it out of her hand, quickly disarming her before she could think twice about her actions. Now that I had her gun, she tensed up in fear. She probably expected me to use it on her, but instead, I emptied the magazine and placed the useless weapon on my desk.

"You want the truth?" I asked her. "Fuck it... Here's the truth..."

Sky relaxed a little as she waited for me to continue.

"I'm in love with you," I confessed. It felt like a weight had been lifted after I poured out my heart. I felt lighter and a bit relieved—but Sky, obviously, didn't feel the same.

Her face took on a myriad of expressions. At first, she looked shocked, then angry, then confused. I knew now was a fucked up time to admit it, but if it would get me exonerated, I would gladly put all my cards on the table. I couldn't have this girl thinking I was responsible for putting her child in a hospital—or even worse, in his grave.

I took a step toward her and she took an immediate step back—like she was scared of me. My love went unreciprocated, and that shit left me feeling some type of way. "So, I take you don't feel the same," I murmured.

Sky shot me a nasty look. "Of course not! Your ass is old enough to be my father! The fuck!" she said with an attitude.

Hearing her say that shit instantly set me off and I quickly went from 0 to 100. "So that's what you think about whenever you see me? That I'm old enough to be your fuckin' father?! You've never saw me as a man with potential? Ever?" I asked, hurt. I had definitely looked at her as more than just a daughter —even though she was the exact same age as Halee.

Sky looked disgusted. "Fuck no!"

Gritting my teeth in anger, I snatched her lil' ass up and squeezed her arm until she winced in pain. "It's that thievin' ass muthafucka Rebel, isn't it? You're in love with his ass, aren't you?"

"My feelings for Rebel have nothing to do with you!" she said through clenched teeth. "Now get the fuck off of me!"

I was so damn mad, I wasn't thinking clearly and before I knew it, I started choking her ass right there in the office.

"You know what? I should put you in the ground with that nigga!" I seethed.

As a man who'd been betrayed by three people I thought I could trust, I no longer felt the urge to give muthafuckas the benefit of the doubt. That shit was over and done with. I refused to be gullible and naive. That shit had cost me more than just a few hundred thousand dollars. It had cost me my sanity and my ability to trust again. Now, I was on some cutthroat ruthless shit! No more Mr. Nice Guy. No more Mr. Laid Back and Accepting.

It was time I started acting like the future CEO of the Kasabian Cartel. Not some soft ass pushover boss. Being that way would only get me taken advantage of at every turn. After the way Sky and Rebel played me, I finally began to understand why my father was as barbaric as he was. You simply couldn't be nice to people.

Sky's eyes bulged in their sockets and she desperately clawed at my hands to release her. But the more she struggled, the harder I squeezed.

"I just knew there was some shit goin' on between ya'll asses!" I yelled. "I ain't good enough for yo ass, but you'll gladly taken a married nigga with mental issues! That's what the fuck you're tellin' me?!" Tightening my grip on her throat, I shook her violently and watched as tears poured down her cheeks.

Blinded by rage and envy, I slammed her face down onto the desk and positioned myself behind her.

"All those months of tryin' to be nice to you! And for what?!" I spat, mushing her face into the hard surface. "Fuck it! If you won't give me what I want, I'll just take it from your ass!"

Sky tried to fight me off but I was much stronger as I pinned her down and snatched her pants down. I didn't give a fuck about the bloodstains on her clothes. She was really gonna be bleeding after I finished with her ass. This bitch had played me one too many times. Then on top of that, she refused to return my affection. She even laughed in my face when I told her I loved her. The bitch had a lot of nerve for someone who had stolen from me without remorse. Where did she get off acting all high and mighty?

"Guess I'll finally get to see if this shit is better than your mom's," I whispered in her ear. She tensed up beneath me as I unzipped my pants. "You know me and Heaven used to fuck all the time. Any chance we got. When I close my eyes, I can still remember how it felt to be deep in her guts... I even put a baby in her once," I bragged.

Sky tried to run, but I grabbed her arm and twisted it behind her back, causing her to howl in pain.

"I bet it's just as good," I whispered in her ear. "So good that I'll probably end up nutting in this sweet, lil' pussy too." I rubbed my hard ass dick against her, but I didn't stick it in just yet. I wanted to fuck with her mentally first—like how she'd fucked with me after telling me I was too damn old for her.

I lined my dick up with her vagina and rubbed my head against her outer pussy lips. They were so damn soft, I almost came prematurely. I was just about to stick it in when I suddenly had a change of heart.

Putting my stiff dick away, I grabbed a handful of her hair and roughly pulled her to her feet. "You know what? I got somethin' better in mind," I said to her.

PTHU!

Sky spat on me, but I didn't bother wiping it off. Instead, I just smiled at her and licked the spit off my lips. "You're gonna pay me back every fuckin' cent you took from me! Every fuckin' penny!" I told her. "You scammed me out of fifteen G's in a single month and you've been working for me for two years. If you managed to steal that much from me every month, then that would mean you owe me nearly four hundred thousand dollars—*plus* interest," I added angrily.

"I don't have that kind of money to pay back!" she yelled.

"Bitch, that ain't my fuckin' problem!" I told her. "Your ass had better come up with my money! All $450,000!" I tightened my grip on her hair. "'Cuz if you don't, you won't have to worry about burying your son! I'll put both you muthafuckas in a box!" And with that, I finally released her and watched her run out of my office in tears. "Stupid bitch," I mumbled under my breath.

7

FLEX

A few days had passed after giving that nigga Rebel the whole clip and I decided to stop by my dad's place to holla at him before he got any calls from anyone else. I wanted him to hear the truth from me before he heard it from someone in the streets. I figured the blow to his pride would be less devastating.

The picture of me and Fatima was spreading like wildfire, and I knew it was only a matter of time before word got back to him. My father, a devoted Christian and relentless Bible-thumper, frowned upon anything he didn't consider "godly."

In spite of the jacked up way I had turned out, my father was a good man and he'd raised me himself—even though he could be overly judgmental at times. I'd never once seen him hit a female or disrespect a man. Honestly, I didn't know who I'd inherited my fucked up ways from. Probably my mom. Unfortunately, I never had the chance to get to know Ma Dukes because she booked right after I was born. I was still bitter about that shit.

It was around 9:15 a.m. when I pulled up to his ranch-style home in Ventura. His car was parked out front so I knew he was at the crib. The nigga was a homebody and he only left to get groceries.

After parking behind his candy red 1976 Camaro, I climbed out and jogged up to his front door and knocked. Several minutes passed and I immediately grew impatient. Ringing the doorbell twice, I waited for him to answer but he never came.

"Pops!" I called out. "Aye, pops?!"

Still no answer.

"Pops?"

Skipping down the stairs, I rounded the house and peered into his bedroom window. My heart dropped to the pit of my stomach when I saw him lying face down on the floor, his body already in the early stages of decomposition.

"POPS?!"

Looking around frantically, I spotted a brick on the ground, grabbed it, and launched it at his window.

KSSSHHHHH!

Glass sprayed everywhere and I cut myself on the arm climbing through it, but my injuries were the least of my worries.

As soon as I was inside, the smell of rotting flesh smacked me in the face. There was no telling how long my father had been deceased, but if I had to guess I'd say a few days at most. "Pops..." I croaked out, gently touching his stiff body. I wanted to hold him, but he was in no condition for all that.

Mustering up what little strength I had, I called an ambulance and waited next to my father's dead body until they arrived. I was so shocked by his death that I could barely process my grief. I just sat there in silence, no tears, no words, nothing. I could hardly even talk as I tried to explain to an EMT what had happened.

Apparently, he'd died of a heart attack, which inadvertently saved me from having to tell him that his only son was gay. Maybe if he'd heard it from me, he would've died from a heart attack anyway. Knowing my old man, he would've been crushed. He felt like anything that wasn't conventional or traditional was a sin.

After discovering my dad's body and giving the police my statement, I was bandaged up and sent on my way. I desperately needed to get back to my place to regroup. I needed time to process everything. I still couldn't believe my pops was gone, but perhaps this was karma for all the shit I'd done throughout the years. I had cheated on my girl, lied to my boss, and murdered in cold blood. Maybe this was my punishment.

My father always said, "You reap what you sow," and now, those words felt like a curse I couldn't escape.

An hour and a half later, I finally made it to Inglewood and when I got to my crib, I pulled into the driveway and just sat there for several moments. I fired up a blunt, turned on some oldies, and just thought about my dad and the positive impact he'd had on my life.

After collecting myself, I climbed out of my girl's car and headed for the door. I didn't even have a chance to stick my key in it before it swung open. As usual, Zuri started going in on my ass.

"Nigga, where the fuck you been at?!" she yelled. "If yo faggot ass was somewhere laid up with Fatima, you should've kept yo stankin' ass there!"

I wasn't in the mood to argue with her messy ass, so I walked past her toward the bathroom to avoid confrontation. I needed a shower to clear my head—but Zuri was hot on my heels, still interrogating me about my whereabouts.

"So you just gon' ignore me, nigga?!" she snapped. "See, that's what you not gon' do!"

This bitch is really wearing me down, I thought to myself.

I had just lost my father. I needed peace—some kind of consolation. But instead, all Zuri could give a nigga was grief! I was done with her bullshit. I'd had it up to here!

As Zuri kept going on and on, I replayed my last conversation with Tommie in my head—it had been five days ago. He wanted me to kill Zuri for stealing from him. At the time, I didn't think I had it in me.

But right now...

"I am so sick of your dusty ass!" she yelled, mushing me in the head. "You think just 'cuz you make a couple dollars now you can do whatever the fuck you want?! Guess what, though?! You're still the same broke, lame ass, dookie dick nigga you've always been! Ain't no coins gon' change that shit, with ya bum ass! You might as well take your raggedy ass back to Fatima!" she shouted. "I hope that ugly ass bitch gives you AIDS!"

Suddenly, I just snapped and started strangling her stupid ass. "BITCH, YOU MUST REALLY WANNA DIE TODAY!" I yelled with tears in my eyes.

Zuri jammed her long ass nails into my eyes and I quickly came back to reality. "Are you fucking crazy?!" she asked in between coughs.

I dropped to my knees and stared at the floor, eyes stinging from her poking me with those fucking stiletto nails.

"I been calling your dumb ass all day to tell you Chosen got shot! And you got the nerve to be mad at me?! I'm the one who should be tight! Me and Sky needed you and you were nowhere to be found!" Zuri shouted in a raspy tone.

"My dad..." I choked out.

"What about him?" Zuri asked with an attitude.

"He's... he's dead..."

Zuri gasped and covered her mouth. "Oh...baby... Oh my God..." She quickly rushed to my side and held me. "I'm so sorry, baby. I'm so sorry! I didn't know!"

Holding her tight, I cried like a fucking baby, and in that moment of vulnerability, I realized that I could never bring myself to kill Zuri. Her ass was the love of my life. Zuri was my entire world.

8

SKY

After a tense but brief standoff with Tommie, I found myself driving around the city, in an attempt to clear the cobwebs from my head. I was all fucked up after all the shit I'd gone through. I even pulled up in Compton to buy a gun before confronting Tommie. A bitch wasn't even thinking straight. And I still couldn't wrap my mind around what Tommie had said back in his office. What the fuck did he mean by *I should put yo ass in the ground with that nigga*?

Did something happen to Rebel?

Was that the reason I hadn't heard back from him?

I'd sent him several text messages and left him a voicemail, and he still had yet to return my call. It wasn't like him. Even though we'd only spent a short amount of time together since reuniting, Rebel had become extremely fond of my son. I just knew when I told him Chosen was in the hospital, he'd come running. Why was he not responding now?

Running a hand through my unkempt hair, I sighed deeply. My life seemed to be falling apart. First, I get fired from Club Allure, then my son gets shot, then I end up owing Tommie close to half a mil, and now I find out that my childhood friend might be dead.

I grew antsy and fearful at the very thought of it. Would Tommie actually kill Rebel? How could he bring himself to hurt his own son-in-law? What happened between them? Did I have anything to do with it?

So many thoughts ran through my mind and before I knew it, I was driving toward Hollywood Hills, where Rebel lived with his family in a hillside mansion. Halfway there, a sudden bout of nausea hit me and I pulled over, jumped out and threw up until my stomach was empty.

Oh fuck!

Please God don't let me be pregnant, too, I prayed.

I told myself that maybe—just maybe—I was sick from all the excitement but I knew better. My body felt the same way it felt before I found out I was pregnant with Chosen. Plus, Rebel and I didn't use any protection that night we'd had sex.

Damn...what else can go wrong?

I wiped my mouth with the back of my wrist, climbed back into my BMW and drove to Rebel's house. When I got to his gated community, I gave the security guard his access code and was permitted entry.

As I pulled up to his hillside manor, the first thing I noticed was the Do Not Cross tape wrapped around the entire property. Clearly, something serious had gone down.

I turned the car around and headed back to the security gate. Pulling up to the entrance, I rolled down my window.

"Hey!" I called out to the security guard.

He set down his Subway sandwich and lumbered toward me, his gruff demeanor on full display. His expression was anything but welcoming.

"What can I do for you?" he asked, his tone dripping with irritation. Clearly, he didn't appreciate me interrupting his meal.

"What happened at 9272 Robin Drive?"

His brows furrowed. "Wow, you didn't hear?" he asked as if I was crazy for not knowing.

"Hear what?" I forced out, voice cracking with emotion. I tried to mentally prepare myself for the bad news to come.

"Someone shot up the place," he said. "When the cops got there, it was a straight-up massacre!"

My heart started beating faster. "They shot up the place?" I repeated.

Tommie's words were on instant replay: *I should put yo ass in the ground with that nigga!*

Was Tommie responsible for this shit?

Did he kill Rebel?

What about his wife?

What about his family?

"Did everyone..." My voice got lodged in my throat and I couldn't bring myself to finish the question. Or maybe I could, but I just didn't want to because I wasn't ready to hear his answer.

"Did everyone what? Did everyone die?" the security guard finished for me.

I couldn't take hearing him say 'yes', so I peeled off before he could answer. "Shit, Rebel! FUCK!" I cursed, punching the center of the steering wheel, causing the horn to blare. "How you gon' knock me up, then leave me? AGAIN!"

My son was in the hospital, my baby daddy may or may not have been alive, and the love of my life had left me alone, while I was more than likely carrying his seed. Could my life get any worse?

Suddenly, my phone started ringing. I prayed that it was Rebel but to my dismay, it was Zuri calling me. "Wassup?" I answered, annoyed.

"*Wassup*?" she repeated with an attitude. "Bitch, where the fuck are you? Chosen is out of surgery."

"You're at the hospital?" I asked, surprised.

"Yes, with Flex. We got here an hour ago. Leilani's here too," she informed me. "Where are you?"

"I told you already, I had to talk to Tommie," I reminded her. "How's Haven?" I asked, like it was her responsibility to know.

"I'm not sure where he is. They won't give me any information on him. They said it's a breach of confidentiality or some shit like that," Zuri explained. "You need to hurry up and get your ass back here. Your son needs you."

"I'm on my way," I told her before hanging up. Then, I said a silent prayer, thanking God that my baby had pulled through. I also prayed for Haven and Rebel to be okay. I didn't want to think about something happening to either of them.

THIRTY MINUTES LATER, I made it to the closest hospital to Rebel's house to see if he had been admitted. I knew I should've gone back to the hospital in Glendale to check on my son, but I wanted to see for myself if Rebel was really dead or not.

Frazzled and exhausted, I walked up to the receptionist at the front desk and asked if she could look up Rebel Coleman in the database.

"No can do," she said with a nonchalant demeanor.

"Excuse me?!" I yelled, ready to crack her in her shit.

"A hospital cannot acknowledge anyone's presence as a patient without specific authorization from the patient or their power of attorney."

"All I want to know is if he's been admitted or not!" I hollered. "What do you mean no can do?! That ain't asking a lot!"

"Ma'am, I'm gonna have to ask you to lower your tone," she said. "Yelling will not make me ignore the hospital's policy."

"Fuck a policy! Let me speak to the fucking manager!"

"Ma'am—"

"I wanna talk to someone that can help me!" I hollered, causing several people to look my way.

"Ma'am, he's just going to tell you the same thing I did."

"Fuck it! Fuck it!" I threw my hands up in the air defenselessly. "I'm leaving!" I said, storming off. "Thanks for nothing!" I tossed over my shoulder.

After my fruitless endeavor of finding Rebel, I hightailed it to the Glendale Memorial Hospital where Chosen and Haven were currently being cared for. I found Zuri, Flex, and Leilani in the waiting room, and Leilani looked as if she hadn't stopped crying since she got the news. Her face was red and puffy, and her eyes were filled with tears.

I walked up to her and hugged her, and Zuri rubbed my back while Flex stood off to the side with a sad look on his face. "What's up with him?" I asked Zuri. He seemed to be taking the news harder than any of us. I had never seen him look so depressed.

"He just found his father's dead body a few hours ago," she informed me.

"Oh...oh my God," I gasped. "That shit must've been terrible." Breaking away from Leilani, I walked over to Flex and hugged him tightly. Despite our differences, we held each other for several, tear-jerking moments, silently comforting each other during our time of need.

Suddenly, Chosen's doctor walked into the room and we all stood with baited breath, awaiting his verdict. "Hi there. May I ask who's the mother?"

I slowly stepped forward. "That would be me..."

Zuri and Leilani stepped forward, as well. "Give it to us straight, Doc," Zuri said.

Leilani nodded in agreement.

The doctor pulled off his glasses and pinched the bridge of his nose, and my stomach dropped. I feared the worst.

"Well... the severity of the trauma and the damage to his lung required immediate surgery. As you probably know, his left lung collapsed, which made it hard for him to breathe on his own. Because of this, we had to insert a chest tube."

I instantly tensed up at the news and Leilani rubbed my back in comfort.

"Don't worry. It sounds a lot worse than it is. The chest tube only has to stay there for a few days to let the excess air out," he explained. "The good news is, the second bullet only grazed him. We will, however, need to keep him a few weeks to monitor his recovery. We have to make sure that his lungs are working properly once the chest tube is removed."

"Will it cause health problems for him later on down the line?" Zuri questioned.

I was happy as hell that she'd asked. It hadn't even crossed my mind to. Maybe I was wrong about her. Maybe she was still my friend despite ratting me out to Tommie.

"Once a punctured lung has healed, it does not typically cause adverse health effects," the doctor explained.

"Can we see him now?" I anxiously asked.

"Of course. But he's still unconscious. The anesthesia has yet to fully wear off."

"What about Haven?" I asked him.

The doctor raised an eyebrow. "I'm sorry? Haven?"

"His real name is Harvey Walker. He was also brought in last night for gunshot wounds," I told him. "We were all together when it happened."

"Ah. Unfortunately, I am not at liberty to discuss his condition—"

"All we wanna know is if he's alive or not!" Zuri yelled.

"Please..." I begged. "He's the father of my son."

"I understand, but unless you're his wife, legal guardian, or attorney, I am unable to provide details on his case."

"Can you at least tell me if he made it?" I pleaded. "I'll call his parents to come...but please don't make them drive here on pins and needles. They live all the way in San Diego. Please... Tell me something that I can tell them..." I urged.

The doctor exhaled deeply, then put his Ray Bans back onto his face. "He's alive..." he finally revealed.

We all breathed a sigh of relief.

"But his injuries are far more severe than your son's," he continued. "I shouldn't be saying this, but... you might want to tell his family to get here as soon as possible. His chances of survival are around forty percent after undergoing major heart surgery and extensive resection," he said quietly.

My throat grew tight. Tears spilled over my lower lids, blurring my vision. "Oh no." I covered my mouth and started sobbing softly.

"It's gonna be okay," Leilani said, patting my back.

"A forty percent chance is better than no chance," Zuri chipped in.

"Don't worry, Sky. The homie's gon' pull through," Flex added. "The nigga just did a bid," he reminded me. "He's a lot tougher than you think."

They all hugged me as I cried wretchedly. In spite of all the problems me and Haven had, he was still the father of my son. For all I knew, Rebel might've been dead. I couldn't bear the thought of having to bury my baby daddy too.

9

TOMMIE

I was still charged up after my short and strained exchange with Sky, and I wanted to take my frustrations out on someone—anyone. I didn't really expect her to be able to come up with the $450,000. She didn't even have a fucking job! But she would have to figure something out, because if she didn't get me my money that was her ass.

The bitch had me on ten and I couldn't believe I didn't ram her when I had the chance. She had become my obsession after her mother's death and ever since she'd started working for me, all I could think about was fucking her. I still couldn't believe I didn't take advantage when I had the perfect opportunity to.

Because of what she did, I wanted to hurt her just as badly as she'd hurt me, but I figured hitting her pockets would cause far more emotional damage than having my way with her. And if she couldn't come up with the $450,000, then I would kill her, her son, and everybody she ever loved. Raping her just wasn't enough.

When I finally made it back home, I was surprised to find my wife Bethany's car in the driveway. She was finally back from her extended vacation in Hawaii with her friends. Her ass had been gone for weeks, but I did not miss her even a little.

After parking my Rolls Royce Phantom behind her brand-new Range Rover truck, I climbed out and made my way to the entrance and let myself in. "Honey, I'm home!" I called out from the granite entryway.

We lived in a 20-million dollar, one-of-a-kind, state of the art mansion in Hollywood Hills, not too far from Halee's former residence. I had no choice but to move her elsewhere after killing her husband and in-laws. She hadn't spoken to me since.

"Oh, great! You're back!" Bethany smiled, walking into the foyer. She was already dressed with her purse slung over her shoulder. "I need money for a mani-pedi. Plus, I may have sushi at Nobu afterwards, so you can toss in a little extra," she said, as if I were her personal ATM.

We'd been married for what felt like forever and we had two beautiful daughters together. However, we didn't have much else in common, other than the fact that we were both born into wealth. Our marriage was not built on love and commitment, and we'd only gotten hitched because of an arrangement my father had with her dad, who was a former politician.

I had never felt for Bethany what I felt Sky and Heaven, and I was sure she lacked emotional ties to me, as well. The bitch never cared to ask me how my day was, or if I was happy or fulfilled in our marriage. All she cared about was maxing out my Visas and catching flights with her girlfriends.

"What else is new?" I asked, agitated.

"Damn. What's up your ass?" she asked with an attitude.

I looked over at my old, ugly hag of a wife and frowned. I could've lied. I could've spared her from a heartbreak. But I wanted the bitch to hurt just as much I was after my encounter with Sky.

"I confessed my feelings for a woman I've been in love with for years and she rejected me," I told Bethany.

Bethany opened and closed her mouth several times, unable to formulate an adequate response. "What the fuck?!" she yelled. "You did not just stand in my face and say that bullshit!"

I shrugged. "You sound surprised. Don't tell me, after all these years, you actually thought I loved your greedy ass."

"I'm your wife!" she hollered with tears in her eyes. "Why wouldn't I think you love me?!"

"Oh, cut the shit already, Bethany. You've never loved me. You just love the life I give you."

"The life YOU give ME?! Muthafucka, my father was the governor of California! You think this shit impresses me?! You think the couple dollars you throw at me means something?! I come from money! You can't give me a life that I was already accustomed to, jackass! Where the fuck is this shit even coming from?!" she cried. "Have you been screwing around on me?!"

"Would you, honestly, care if I have?" I asked, unenthused. "You're hardly ever home. And when you are, you've always got your hand out. You don't give a fuck about me. You never have."

"Tommie, I love y—"

I grabbed her face and squeezed hard as fuck before she could finish. Shoving her backwards, I slammed her against the hallway wall and stared at her with piercing eyes. "Please, Bethany... I've had a fucked up day. Don't make it any worse by saying some shit you don't mean. We both know how you really feel about me. And that's okay...'cuz I feel the exact same way about your pale, dry pussy having ass. You make me sick, bitch. Every time I look at you, I have a strong urge to vomit. Why the fuck do you think I haven't touched you in years? Not only do I find you unattractive, my dick does too...you selfish, self-centered, greedy cunt."

Bethany shoved me off of her. "FUCK YOU, TOMMIE!" she screamed before running toward the door.

I ran after her and grabbed her by the hair, then slammed her against the wall face first, busting her mouth wide open. Like I said before, I was on some ruthless shit. Being betrayed by people that I loved and cared about had unleashed something dark in me. Something that I had kept hidden deep inside for over fifty years.

"That's the thing, bitch. You don't fuck me at all! You're too busy spending up all my fuckin' money! That's all the fuck you're good for!" I hollered.

"Tommie, stop!" she cried, mouth bleeding profusely as I dragged her toward the bedroom. "I'm sorry!" she said. "I can change!"

Throwing her onto the bed, I pinned her down, ignoring the tears in her eyes and the smeared blood all over her face. Pressing my body against hers, I snatched her dress up and noticed her thighs were shaking and her heart was racing. I didn't know if she was scared or excited, and honestly, I didn't give a fuck. Sky had gotten me all worked up and I had to get this fucking nut off somehow.

Grinding my hard-on against Bethany's pelvis, I reached down and began pulling and pinching on her nipples. She yelped in pain and I leaned down and bit them so hard I left teeth marks.

Instead of telling me to stop, she arched her back giving me easier access, offering them to me.

One of my hands moved to her wet pussy and I began to gently caress her. I was surprised that she was even turned on. But Bethany had always been just as crazy as me, if not more. In no time, she launched into a powerful orgasm, quivering and shaking from the impact of her climax. I really could not believe it. I had bashed her in the face, and now, here she was, squirting against my fingers.

I held her, gently kissing and caressing her as she slowly came down from her high. She was smiling at me, with a face full of blood, looking like an auburn-haired Harley Quinn.

"Oh, Tommie... I do love you," she whispered.

I didn't tell her that I loved her back as I pulled my dick out of my dress pants. I was hard as a rock as I pushed the tip of my cock against her wet pussy lips. Inch by inch, I slowly slid into her, deliberately and without stopping.

With each inch, she gasped, like this was her first time. She was so tight, so warm and so wet, and it wasn't until then that I realized we hadn't fucked in ages. With how tight she was, I knew she hadn't been fucking around on me.

Grabbing her waist, I deepened my thrusts, driving further and further into her, penetrating her cervix.

"Tommie! Not so hard! Slow down!" she cried out. It was obviously hurting her, but I guess you could say I wanted her to experience agony. I didn't wanna be the only one in pain in this fucked up ass marriage of ours.

I ignored her cries as I forced her to adjust to my deep penetration. She wrapped her legs tighter around me and put her hands on my shoulders. In and out, I drilled into her at a strong, deep, steady pace. Before I knew it, she was crying out in ecstasy and I gradually increased my speed.

Bethany's eyes began rolling to the back of her head as I hit places she never imagined I could, and she was writhing in pleasure.

"Fuck me, Tommie!" she screamed.

Her orgasm hit her like a tsunami and I continued to hammer into her until her toes were throwing up gang signs.

I went even deeper and she screamed out in pain—she was so full of my cock that her head was spinning.

"T—Tommie," she stuttered.

"Take this dick, bitch!" I moaned.

She looked up at me and saw the fire in my eyes as she

exploded in a third, mind-blowing orgasm. By then, she was wetter than the Titanic. After today, I could no longer insult the moisture of her womanhood. My bitch was wet as fuck!

She was still getting her bearings when I pulled out and flipped her over. I pulled her onto her knees and slid my hard dick into her sopping snatch and began thrusting all over again.

Reaching a hand under her body, I started playing with her clit, while my other hand gripped her hip. I was pounding into her like a sex-deprived animal and I didn't know how much longer I could last before I nutted deep inside her.

Wrapping her hair around my fist, I pulled her back against me so that her back was pressed against my chest. I was thrusting like a madman as I squeezed her tits, and she was crying out in a pleasure-filled pain. Letting go of her hip, I wrapped my hand around her throat, holding her in place as I fucked her helpless form.

"Oh, shit, Tommie! I'm about to cum again!" She bellowed.

"Ah, fuck! Sky!" I screamed out as I came deep inside my wife.

She tried to pull away from me, but I held her that way for about twenty seconds before finally letting her go.

Bethany fell onto her stomach, then rolled over and shot me an angry glare. "Who the fuck is Sky?!" she yelled.

Before I could answer, my phone started ringing. I climbed off the bed and grabbed it out of the pile of clothes on the floor. It was my chief lieutenant and second-in-command, Darius. "What's up, D?" I answered.

"Sorry to bug you this early, but I've got some shit to tell you that you aren't gonna be too happy to hear," he said.

Bethany folded her arms and rolled her eyes. She was still upset about me calling her Sky but ask me if I gave a fuck.

"What is it?" I asked Darius.

"That nigga Rebel is still alive..." he told me.

My jaw muscle tensed as I gripped the phone tightly against my ear. "How do you know?" I asked him.

"I had my peoples search for his death certificate, but they couldn't locate it in any of the databases in all of the hospitals in LA," he explained.

"You sure there wasn't just some typo? Rebel is a pretty uncommon name," I said, making up some flimsy excuse.

"Trust me, I had them dig through every alias and every corner of this earth. Came up empty," he said, his tone cold and sharp. "That muthafucka's still out here breathing when he shouldn't be."

I ran a hand through my salt and pepper hair. "Then I guess it's time I make sure he stops."

10

REBEL

When I opened my eyes from the dreadful nightmare that held me captive, I saw the last person I expected to see, hovering over me with a look of compassion on her freckled face. "Halee?" I whispered in a barely audible tone. My throat was sore and raspy from having a tube inserted into my body.

Halee leaned down and placed a gentle kiss on my forehead. "Welcome back, baby," she smiled, running her fingers over my locs.

I tried to sit up in bed, but my body was stiff and still aching from being shot. I couldn't move and I was at her mercy, for the time being. "Where am I?" I asked, looking around the sterile room. It didn't look like a hospital. It looked an ordinary bedroom in a house, but there was an IV beside my bed and a heart monitor next to that.

"I brought you to a private medical center in Irvine so that my father wouldn't find you. He still thinks you're dead, but who knows how long that'll last. You know shit gets back to him pretty fast," she explained. "It's only a matter of time before he finds out he didn't kill you."

I looked down at my bandaged torso, then I noticed that my right leg was propped up in a cast. I was alive but in terrible fucking shape—thanks to Tommie and Flex. "My parents..." I said, remembering the tragic events leading up to this very moment.

With tears in her eyes, she reached over and held my hand. "Your dad," she began. "He didn't make it, baby. I'm so sorry."

Damn.

My father...was dead?

"We laid him to rest a couple days ago. You were still in a medically induced coma, so I had to hold the funeral without you," she said. "I'm really sorry, Rebel... I wanted to wait for you, but I couldn't just leave him at the funeral home while you recovered. I had to do what I had to do."

A single tear rolled down my cheek. "You had the funeral without me?" I choked out. Hearing that shit left me feeling angered and helpless. I didn't even get a chance to say a final goodbye to my dad.

"Don't worry, it was a beautiful service," she told me. "Afterwards, I had him cremated and his ashes scattered across the Pacific Ocean, as he requested in his will."

Snot trickled from my nose and Halee rushed to wipe it up. "And my mom?" I asked in a broken voice.

"She survived the attack," Halee said to my relief. "But the doctors said she'll never walk again..."

I blinked and more tears spilled from my eyes. "What...?" I was floored at the news.

"There was severe trauma to her spinal cord. The doctors did all they could for her, but the damage was irreparable," she explained.

I looked down at my hands and noticed they were trembling. Tommie had killed my father, crippled my stepmom, and changed my life forever. I had to clap back at that nigga. There was no way in hell I could let this shit slide.

"Baby... I know what you're thinking. But it's best if you just walk away while you still can. Cut your losses and count your blessings. You do not wanna start a war with my father," she warned me.

"Count my blessings?" I repeated. "Halee... Look at me. Look at what the fuck this nigga did to my family! I can't just walk away from that shit!" I yelled at her.

"Rebel, I'm telling you now... you do not want conflict with my dad," she stressed. "He doesn't even know you're still alive. Let's just move out of the country somewhere. Start over," she proposed. "We'll take Denver with us and I'll pay for her rehabilitation, and find her the best caregiver money can buy. We can still be a family! We can still make this work! We can still be together!"

I snatched my hand away from hers, like it was made of hot coal. "I don't wanna be a fuckin' family, Halee! I don't wanna ride off into the sunset together, pretending your father didn't kill the only nigga that ever cared about me!" More tears slid down my cheeks.

"Rebel, please," she cried. "I don't want anything else to happen to you! I don't wanna see you hurt! I'm the one who found you half-alive! It was hard enough to slip away from my father to make it back to you before you died! I can't risk losing you again! I can't take seeing you like that again. I love you! Don't you love me, too?! Don't you care about leaving me alone?"

"No..."

Halee looked confused. "Wh—what?"

"No... I don't love you," I finally revealed. "I never did. And I would rather die than spend another minute of my fuckin' life acting like I feel somethin' I don't!" I told her. "We don't gotta put on this front no more, Halee. Don't you get it? My fuckin' father is dead," I choked out. "It's a wrap. This game we've been playin' is over..."

Suddenly, she jumped to her feet and pressed her finger into one of my wounds, causing blood to spill out through the stitches. I had staples in my stomach after being shot.

"*Argh!*" I winced in pain. My shit felt like it was on fire.

"It ain't over till I say it's over!" she screamed. "You're still my husband and we're going to make this work, come hell or high water!" she hollered before finally removing her hand. And with that, she stormed out of the room, leaving me to my scattered thoughts.

"Spending time with you...like this...it feels so familiar to me," Sky said as we strolled through the pier.

I couldn't have agreed more. I was consumed by the desire to be with her, to talk to her and have her near me. I could stay here forever with her. No one else existed right now.

"I feel the exact same way," I said. "Whenever I'm with you I feel like I'm home." I felt like I could conquer the world with just one hand, as long as she was holding the other.

I was daydreaming about my final moments with Sky when Halee stormed into my room the following afternoon, carrying a briefcase.

"You claim you don't love me and that you never have... Well then, I suppose there's no need for us to keep up this façade," she hissed, slamming the briefcase down onto my good leg. It still hurt like hell for some odd reason.

As a matter of fact, my entire body was in pain. Not only would my stepmom need rehabilitation. I would probably need it, as well.

"What the fuck is that?" I growled.

Halee opened the briefcase with an attitude and pulled out a thick stack of paperwork. "Divorce papers," she said plainly. "I had them drafted up after I left yesterday. No need to front anymore—like you said, right?" She pulled out a pen and handed it to me.

By the grace of God, she'd had a change of heart.

But I couldn't help but wonder what brought about her change of heart?

Maybe she was finally tired of being in a dead-end marriage too. With this divorce we could both be free. She could finally have a man who reciprocated her love, and even though I didn't Halee, she was still very much deserving of love.

"I need time to look them over," I told her. I trusted her, but I still wanted to make sure everything looked legit.

"No need. You'll get half of all assets," she said. "You can even keep the cars."

I shot her an unamused look. "Fuck the cars. What about the baby?" I asked her.

Halee pursed her lips. "There is no baby," she confessed.

I looked at her ass like she was crazy. "What? Fuck you mean there ain't no baby? You told me you were pregnant."

"I lied," she admitted.

There was a long, tense silence that lingered in the air between us. "Why?"

"Because ever since we've walked down that aisle you've been emotionally detached from me. It got even worse when that bitch Sky came into the picture. I just wanted you to focus on me for once, so I made it all up. I figured a baby could bring us closer."

I shook my head at her, grabbed the pen, and calmly signed my name on the dotted line.

"I'll have the attorney handle everything, including trans-ferring funds to your separate account," she told me.

"So, this is it?" I asked, just to be sure.

"This is it," she said. "And after today, you'll never see me again. But I can't assure you that you won't ever see my father again," she added. "After all, I can't protect a man that doesn't love me," she said, being petty as usual.

"I don't need your protection, Halee. But your forgiveness would be nice."

Halee wiped away her tears. "What the hell am I forgiving you for?" she asked snidely.

"For not doing this shit sooner," I said.

11

BLADE

"*WAAAAAHHH!!! WAAAAAHHH!!! WAAAAAHHH!!!*" AJ hollered at the top of his lungs as Jessica bounced him on her hip. She was warming up his bottle on the stove top as me and Smurf sat at the kitchen table, discussing the logistics of our new drug operation. Now that Haven was out of the equation, I needed someone else to sell off the block I planned on buying.

"So you know a nigga I can cop a brick from?" I asked Smurf as I rolled up a 'wood.

"Yeah, some Armenian nigga named Tommie. My nigga Beezy just bought a block from him not too long ago. Nigga said he got the best white in town. Son gotta pay him a percentage though. He said it's something like a partnership."

"A percentage?! Why the fuck I gotta pay this nigga a percentage? Why can't I just buy the white and sell it off?"

"*WAAAAAHHH!!! WAAAAAHHH!!! WAAAAAHHH!!!*" AJ continued to scream like someone was trying to kill him.

"Damn, bae, you couldn't just put that shit in the microwave?!" I snapped at Jessica. "You see we in here politickin'."

I could've killed that hoe for taking my money and running off with my son, but I forgave her for the simple fact that I knew I'd pushed her to that point. I had cheated on her, sent her to work at the same club as my side bitch, and pretty much gave her every reason not to trust me. It wasn't easy letting bygones be bygones, but I had to be the bigger person. For our son.

"It's dangerous to microwave a baby's bottle! It could scald his mouth!" she shot back.

I ran a hand over my brush waves in frustration and tried my best to ignore his incessant whining. "He got the best white in town though?" I asked for verification.

"The best, my nigga." Smurf pulled a small vial of cocaine out of his pocket and passed it to me.

I opened it and dumped a little on the back of my wrist, then snorted it off. "Damn, this shit really is official," I said, wiping at my nostrils.

Jessica immediately started going in. "*Unh-unh*, nigga! Don't be doing that shit in front of my baby!"

"If you get the fuck outta the kitchen, he won't have to see it!" I yelled at her.

Jessica snatched the bottle out of the pot on the stove and stormed out of the room with an attitude.

Bitches, I thought to myself. *Can't live with 'em, can't live without 'em.*

"So, how do I get in contact with this Tommie cat?" I asked Smurf.

AFTER SMURF LEFT and Jess laid AJ down for the night, I met her in the bedroom, where she was casually wrapping her hair to tie it down with a scarf.

"Is that going to be your new side hustle now? Selling

drugs?" she asked with her back facing me. "Because if it is, you haven't asked me how I feel about that," she said.

"I didn't think I had to," I said matter-of-factly.

"If you plan on having that shit around my son, then you definitely need to run it by me first."

"You know what, Jess? I'm getting real sick and tired of you thinkin' you run shit! If I'mma be the one takin' care of everything and payin' all the bills, why the fuck would I need your approval?!"

"Because this is *my* house! And I don't want that shit under *my* roof!" she yelled.

"If you gon' be on this my, my, my shit, then we may as well say fuck getting married," I told her. "Marriage is about putting away selfishness and taking on the concept of teamwork."

Jessica softened at my words.

Slowly walking over toward her, I gently cupped her face. "Look, I love you, baby. And we in this shit together now. Arguing ain't gon' get us nowhere."

"I love you t—"

Before she could finish, my tongue was in her mouth.

Backing up against the bed, I fell down and she aggressively removed my pants. After freeing my dick, she stuffed it into her mouth, drooling on my shaft, sporadically deep-throating as much of me as she could. This was why I loved Jessica. Her head game was fucking fire.

Grabbing her by the hair, I lifted her head so that we were eye level. "I really do love your ass, Jess. But if you ever try to skip town on me again, I'll bury your fuckin' ass..."

THE NEXT DAY, I made some calls and had some friends of friends put together a meeting with me and the infamous Tommie Kasabian. We met at the rooftop bar of the Ace Hotel, and I wasn't at all surprised to see he was surrounded by a team of enforcers. He was a lion at the head of the food chain. Since the nigga didn't know me from Adam, I understood why he needed to take extra precaution.

With his black Armani suit and greasy, slicked back hair, Tommie fit the typical stereotype of a mafia boss. He had ivory skin, dark, sunken in eyes, a round belly and eight fingers.

Swaggering over to his table, I extended my hand for him to shake but he just looked at it like it was covered in shit. The dreaded cat beside him snickered, and I did an automatic double-take when I realized who he was.

Flex?

We didn't know each other personally, and we didn't hang in the same circle. And the only reason I recognized him was because I'd seen him on Zuri's Instagram. Unbeknownst to Sky, I had peeked at her friend's page a couple times because I thought she was cute and thick as fuck. If she didn't already have a man, I might've gotten at her.

I started to say something to his ass but Tommie interrupted me. "I only shake hands with men I intend to do business with," he said in an uppity ass tone. "And I'm not quite sure if I plan to do business with you. So why don't you sit down and tell me why, exactly, I should."

Dropping my hand at my side, I sat down at the table and cleared my throat. He left me feeling rejected and small after ignoring my warm gesture. I wasn't the type of nigga that shook hands either, so I was already out of my element.

"Recently, I came up on a lil' bread. I wanna use it to make an investment and I heard you were the nigga to come see, so here I am."

Tommie cocked his head to the side. "How much bread we talkin', kid?" he asked.

"Twenty-five G's," I told him.

Tommie smirked, then reached down and grabbed his glass

of whiskey. It wasn't until then that I noticed he had an entire bottle in front of him. I wanted to help myself but he hadn't offered, and I was too intimidated to ask after the way he had shitted on me earlier.

"My shit normally goes for thirty," he said. "But I think we can work somethin' out."

I damn near leapt out of my seat and kissed his ass out of gratitude. I needed a win after everything I'd gone through. "Really? Man, that's wassup!" I said excited and with a huge smile on my face. I was still in disbelief at his immediate acceptance of my offer.

"As long as you give me fifty percent of all profits," he added on the sly.

"Fifty percent?!" I repeated. Smurf told me I'd have to give him a cut, but he didn't say shit about 50%.

"Damn right, fifty percent. I can't have cats out here selling dirt in my territory. In case you didn't know it, I got the city on smash," he boasted. "And if you ain't an ally, you're an enemy. Plain and simple. So what's it gonna be? Your ass already took up enough of my time. Do we gotta deal or not? Are you an ally or an enemy?"

I didn't like the idea of giving him half of my profits, but it was looking like I didn't have any other choice. Haven was out of the equation and I had to get the drugs from someone. Plus, it didn't make sense to buy a brick if I couldn't move it. I didn't have that type of clientele. Niggas knew my cousin. They didn't know me.

"Would you consider lowering the percentage if I moved more coke?" I asked him. I wasn't no work horse.

Tommie narrowed his eyes at me. "*Hmm*," he pondered on my offer. "I'll consider it," he said. "Can you move a bird? A whole bird?" he asked me doubtfully.

"Trust me, I make them pigeons disappear like a magician," I bragged. Honestly, I didn't know the first thing about selling drugs but luckily, I had Smurf to help me out. That nigga was known for keeping the fiends fed.

"Only sell what they need 'cuz them fiends will sell what they don't smoke in a heartbeat," Tommie informed me.

I fronted like I knew that already. "One more thing," I added. "Shit been rough for a nigga lately," I told him. "I got niggas out here lookin' to take my head off about this bread. If you can guarantee me protection, then you got yourself a deal."

Tommie tossed his shot of whiskey back and smiled. "Kid, my allies are more than just friends. They're family. And nobody fucks with my family," he stressed. "As long as you're piecing me off every month, you can rest assured that nobody's gonna fuck with you. I can guarantee you that."

I extended my hand again and this time, he shook it. "Say less."

No longer would I have to worry about Haven's peoples seeking vengeance for his shooting. His folks knew that it was me who blew at him. The streets talked. But now that me and Tommie had joined forces, I wouldn't have to look over my shoulder 24/7. And I could drink at a bar without having to worry about a gang of Bloods running up on me.

Shit was finally starting to look up.

This was my time to shine.

12

SKY
THREE WEEKS LATER

I 'd been letting Haven's parents stay at my place while they were in town, and as always, it was a challenge dealing with them. They were demanding, hard to get along with, and they bitched about every little thing. I couldn't even say it was due to their son being in the hospital because they were always like that. Fake bougie and extremely bothersome. They acted like their child was the only one who'd gotten shot. They weren't the only ones who'd come close to losing their only son.

To our relief, Haven had quickly recovered from his injuries and his survival rate went from 40% to 100%! No one was happier than me to learn that my baby daddy was gonna live! However, he and Chosen had to remain in the hospital's care for several weeks for monitoring and rehabilitation. I had also signed up Chosen for regular counseling sessions but he hated it, and I had to bribe him with his Nintendo Switch just to get him to go.

Me and Haven's parents had decided to throw a welcome home party for our sons since they were getting discharged the same day, and Leilani was nice enough to come with me while I picked them up. Plus, it gave me an excuse to get away from Haven's annoying ass parents.

They complained about everything! The way I cooked, the way I cleaned my house, my basic cable package—they even complained about the fucking furniture, calling my bed cheap and uncomfortable—even though I'd let them sleep in my room while I slept in Chosen's bed. I didn't understand them. If they hated it at my place so much, why didn't they just get a damn hotel room somewhere?

"Girl, I've had it up to here with Haven's folks," I told Leilani on the way to the hospital. "Them muthafuckas are getting on my last nerves."

"Well, thank God you only have to deal with them for a few more days."

"Yessss!" I sighed dramatically. A few days couldn't come fast enough. "They'll be back in San Diego and out of my hair, and I'll finally have my place back to myself!"

"So, have you heard from Rebel?" Leilani asked out of the blue.

I thought about my childhood friend and that dreadful day I discovered his home surrounded in Do Not Cross tape. I thought about the security guard telling me that a massacre had occurred. I had searched for articles online about it and even watched the news religiously, but no one had reported the incident. If there really was in fact a shooting, then someone had worked hard to cover it up. I was still convinced that someone was Tommie, based on the things he'd said in his office.

"Nope. Nothing. I even stopped by his job, but no one had seen or heard from him in weeks. I'm starting to think he really is d—"

"Don't say it!" Leilani cut me off. "Don't even speak that shit into existence."

Before I could argue with her logic, we pulled up to the entrance of Glendale Memorial Hospital.

"Go ahead. I'll find somewhere to park," Leilani told me.

After collecting my family and signing the discharge paperwork, we all made our way back to my place. Haven was unusually quiet but Chosen hadn't shut up since he got in the car. Despite coming so close to death, he was still just as buoyant and talkative as he'd always been, and he couldn't wait to get back to his video games.

I hadn't thought much about the identity of the shooters since I had accused Tommie of being the perpetrator. Nor had I mentioned our altercation to Haven. To be honest, I simply wanted to move on with my life. Not play detective. Whoever pulled the trigger that day would get their karma eventually. It always came back full circle.

As soon as we parked in the designated space in front of my apartment building, Chosen jumped out of the car and sprinted to the front door. The rehabilitation had done wonders for him. Haven, however, was moving slower than a snail.

"You alright, babe?" I asked him.

He slung an arm around my shoulders and pulled me close to him. "Yeah, I'm good, love bug," he said before kissing the top of my head. "Just glad to be up out that bitch."

Me, Leilani and Haven stopped at the front door and I slowly unlocked it. "WELCOME HOME!!!" everyone screamed, surrounded by balloons and gifts. Haven's parents, Zuri, Flex, and a few of his boys from our old hood were there.

"Presents!!!" Chosen exclaimed. *Mommy, can I open them*, he signed.

"You don't wanna eat first?" I asked him, twisting my fingers to communicate with him.

Chosen anxiously shook his head no.

"Fine. You can open them," I said, caving to his demands per usual. That's why he was so damn spoiled now.

Chosen ran off to open his gifts and Haven's parents hugged their son like it was their first time seeing him in decades. "Oh, baby, look at you," his mother, Pamela said, rubbing his cheek. "You've lost so much weight. We're gonna have to stay an extra week just to fatten you back up!"

Like hell you are, I thought to myself.

"There's no way you'll put your weight back on with Sky's terrible ass cooking," she added.

Nobody's forcing you to eat it, bitch. That's what I wanted to say, but instead I bit my tongue—and believe me, it hurt like hell.

"Man, that hospital food was nasty as fuck," Haven chuckled. "And you ain't been terrorizing my woman while I was gone, have you?" he asked his mom.

"Yes!" I said, butting in. "Terrorizing is the perfect word for it!"

Haven grabbed me, pulled me towards him and held me. "Ma, you can't be comin' sideways at my girl," he told her. "You know this gon' be yo future daughter-in-law, right?"

Pamela curled her lips. Her old ass had never liked me. As a matter of fact, none of my old boyfriends' moms did. Even Denver despised me.

"Daughter-in-law?" Pamela narrowed her eyes at me and took the news with grim acceptance.

She clearly didn't like the way that shit sounded at all. She never even wanted me to be the mother of his child. She always felt like I wasn't good enough for Haven. But Chosen was here and he wasn't going anywhere, and despite the way she felt about me, she loved my son unconditionally.

"That's right." Haven took my hand and gradually got down onto one knee. It was evident that he was still healing from his injuries because everything he did seemed to be in slow motion. "I love you with everything in me, baby. And every day that I sat in that cage, I thought about you and our son, and our future together. I done already wasted five years to the system and I don't wanna waste another minute of my life without you. Baby…" He looked up into my eyes and smiled. "It's like we've known each other forever. They say every king needs a queen and I know I've found my queen in you. I love our vibe, and I just want you to know you got me and I'mma do everything in my power to meet your expectations. I'm on you like icing on a cake and I'm ready to spend the rest of my days with you. Sky Marie Thompson, will you marry me, baby?"

Everyone waited on pins and needles, and some of the guests even pulled their phones out to video record my response. It was such a touching moment and I felt like I was on the verge of having a panic attack. Haven knew how much I hated being put on the spot. Even Chosen was standing there with his mouth hanging wide open. None of us could've predicted this twist.

"Haven…" A tear rolled down my cheek as I struggled to finish my sentence. "I—I…"

Haven looked confused.

"I can't because I…"

Haven's brows knitted together in anger. "Because you what?!" he growled, getting irate.

"I can't tell you right here in front of everybody," I squeaked out.

"Why the hell not?!" he demanded to know. "You done already embarrassed the fuck outta me in front of everybody!"

Pamela suddenly stepped forward to calm him down. "Honey, I think you should—"

"Stay the fuck outta this, Ma! This ain't got shit to do with you!" Haven said, pointing a finger in her face.

His dad looked ready to crack his head open, but he kept

his mouth closed. His parents were scared of his ass but they *loved* to torment me.

"Why the fuck can't you marry me, huh?!" Haven screamed, spraying saliva all over my face. "What? I ain't good enough or somethin'? Why don't you wanna spend forever with me?!"

I dissolved into tears. "Because I'm pregnant with another man's baby!" I cried, causing everyone in the room to gasp.

13

REBEL

"Well, this is it," I said in an apathetic tone as me and my step-mom stood in the living room of a brand-new condo in downtown Long Beach that overlooked the city. Technically, I was the only one standing—with the assistance of a cane, that is. My mother was in an electric foldable wheelchair and she would remain in one for the rest of her life. "It certainly ain't the Ritz..."

With an uneager look on her face, she wheeled herself over toward the floor-to-ceiling windows. Thanks to the settlement, I had a nice, lil' cushion but I couldn't blow through the money like I wanted, because I had a couple moves to make first. So instead of buying some big fancy house on the hills, I opted for a small but spacious 2-bedroom apartment near the beach.

"I guess this will do," Denver said nonchalantly. She'd been in a shitty ass mood ever since we were discharged from the medical center. "It's no mansion in Hollywood Hills, that's for sure," she griped.

"We'll get there, Ma. But for now, let's just be grateful that we got a roof over our heads and breath in our lungs," I told her. Halee could've been petty as fuck. She could've made it to where I didn't get shit out of the divorce. After all, that money belonged to her father. Every dollar, every cent.

"Don't talk to me about gratitude. My husband is dead," Denver reminded me for the hundredth time.

Maintaining my patience, I walked over to her and kneeled down in front of her chair. Grabbing the handles, I carefully turned her towards me, so that she had no choice but to look me in the eyes. "But we aren't," I reminded her. "And *that* is somethin' to be grateful for. A wise person once told me to rejoice always, pray continually, and give thanks in all circumstances." Honestly, it was some shit I heard Sky say once but my stepmom didn't need to know all that.

"*Tuh*!" Denver snorted in disgust. "Save your biblical bullshit for someone else. You know I've never been into that man-made religious crap," she said in a nasty tone.

I stood to my feet, walked over to my duffel bag, and pulled out a King James bible. I made my way back over to my stepmom and tossed it in her lap. "Maybe it's time ya ass start," I said before turning on my heel. I'd started reading it myself during my brief stint in the hospital. A second chance at life had suddenly made me move differently.

Grabbing my duffel bag, I disappeared inside my bedroom. The condo was minimally furnished. It had the basics; two beds, a couple dressers, a futon in the living room. If I wanted to pimp it out then I would have to spend a bag, and I wasn't trying to spend any unnecessary money. At least, not right now. I had too much shit to take care of.

Unzipping my duffel bag, I pulled out a 9A-91, a compact assault rifle with an attached scope. I also had a Glock 17, an M4 and an F9 that would knock a nigga's heart out his chest.

So much for being godly.

In spite of Halee's warning, I wasn't running, I wasn't ducking, and I wasn't going to forget what Tommie took from me. I was going to stay right in LA and strategize. I couldn't let that nigga get away with what he did. I didn't give a fuck how many people he had on his payroll. I had plenty for any nigga that wanted it.

After laying the guns out on my mattress, I loaded a fresh magazine into each of them. Next, I pulled out a bulletproof vest. As soon as I could walk without the use of my cane, I planned to go after the entire Kasabian Cartel—starting with that old ass bitch Thomas Sr. I knew in my heart that he was responsible for the murder of Sky's parents and I couldn't let him go unpunished either.

Sky...

At the thought of her, I shed a little animosity and I couldn't help but wonder what her life was like without me. Was she happy? Did she miss me? Did she think about me half as much as I thought about her?

Now that I was divorced, I planned to pursue her with renewed determination. But I couldn't focus on a future with her until I tied up the loose ends from my past. I had to get at them niggas Tommie and Flex before I even thought about calling Sky. I refused to put her life in jeopardy while there was more than likely a price tag on my head.

A few days ago, Halee sent me a text—despite promising me that I'd never hear from her again—and she warned me that her father had niggas looking for me. She begged me to leave town and even offered to buy me a one-way ticket but I turned her down. LA was home and it always would be. I wasn't about to let her hoe ass daddy run me out of my own city.

Taking a seat on the edge of my bed, I pulled a small bag of coke out the duffel bag and dumped the contents onto the nightstand. Using my credit card to cut the powder into several fine lines, I snorted up a generous amount and waited for its effects.

My mom didn't know that I had started using again. It was a nasty habit that I'd sworn off and I had kept my promise—until my father was murdered in cold blood. My only living relative. His death had made me run right back to the addictive substance. You see, I suffered severe depression and anxiety after losing my birth mother to cancer and the drugs helped to numb the pain. I ended up kicking the habit with counseling and anti-depressants, but I doubted therapy could remedy the hurt I felt from losing my father. The shit was too much for me to bear. And it was fucked up too because I hadn't touched the shit in five years. Now, I couldn't go five minutes without a hit.

"Rebel!" Denver called out.

I quickly swiped the coke back into the baggy and tossed it in the top drawer of my nightstand. If my stepmom found out I was using again and plotting to take down Tommie and his crew, she'd be so disappointed in me. And with everything she had been through, the last thing I wanted to do was disappoint her.

"Yeah, Ma?" I asked, closing my bedroom door behind me.

"I'm hungry," she said, wheeling herself towards the kitchen. "Is there anything for me to cook in the cabinets?"

"Nah, but I can order us takeout."

"I don't want takeout!" she yelled. "I want a home-cooked meal. I want our catering team! I want my husband! And I want my old life back!" she shouted before breaking down in tears.

I rushed to her side and held her.

"I miss Robert!" she wept, falling apart at the seams.

She could no longer hold it together. Her mask had cracked, revealing the pain and hurt underneath. She had tried to be a G and remain strong, considering the circumstances. She hadn't even shed a tear when I told her that Halee buried Dad without us. Denver's tough girl act had finally disintegrated, exposing her vulnerability.

"I know, Ma." Somehow, we had to figure out how to put the pieces of our life back together. The patriarch figure in our family was gone now and one way or another, we had to learn how to live without him—regardless of how difficult that may have been.

"I miss him so much, Rebel! I miss him so much! It's not fair!"

"I know, Ma... I miss him too," I said, choking back tears.

I couldn't wait to make that nigga Tommie suffer. Karma was coming for his ass, full force.

14

FLEX

"Damn. Can you believe Sky is really pregnant?" Zuri asked me after Sky's welcome home/failed engagement party. "I thought she looked a lil' fat these days. Now I finally know why."

We'd just walked through the door of our house, and I wanted to shower and roll a blunt. Not hear more shit about Sky and all her drama. Zuri had talked about her on the entire ride back to the crib and right about now, I just wanted to purge myself of Sky. Her bullshit didn't have shit to do with me. She was Haven's problem, not mine. A nigga had his own dilemmas to deal with.

"C'mon, bae, kill that shit already," I sighed.

Once Zuri started on one of her rants about Sky, it was hard to get her to shut the fuck up. "I'm just mad she didn't tell me first! We spent damn near everyday working together! You'd think it would've crossed her mind to tell me. What type of friend keeps a secret like that?"

To be so damn judgmental, Zuri was the queen of keeping secrets herself. Sky didn't even know she was born a man until recently.

"Last I checked, ya'll weren't friends at all. I guess that lil' incident with Haven and Chosen brought ya'll back together, huh?"

"You know that's my girl. You know I can't stay mad at her ass for too long. I've already appointed myself as the god-mother of her future daughter." Zuri gave me a big, goofy ass grin. "Oh my God! Speaking of which, what if she has a little girl?!" she exclaimed. "I'mma riot if she doesn't name her after me!"

I wasn't trying to hear her talk about Sky all night, so I decided to dip. "Aye, I got some shit I need to handle for Tommie," I lied. "You need anything while I'm out?"

Zuri pouted, but she didn't argue with me about leaving like she usually did. Now that I was paying all the bills and doing everything a man should do, she'd decided to cut me some slack. She also could've been taking it easy on me because of my father's untimely death. Either way, I was thankful for her falling the fuck back. That begging shit got exhausting after a while.

"No," she murmured.

I could tell there was more she wanted to say but chose not to.

Pulling a knot out of my pocket, I tossed it on the end table. "Go do somethin' nice for yaself," I said before leaving.

After leaving her to her own devices, I drove to Artesia, where Fatima lived. I'd been meaning to pay her ass a visit, but planning my father's funeral had set me back. I hadn't forgotten the shit she did. The way she had exposed me was foul as fuck. I still had niggas clowning me about the photo that went viral on the Gram.

Parking in front of her small, two-story home, I climbed out of Zuri's car, grabbed my burner, and tucked it in my waist. There was a suppressor screwed on the end, so if I squeezed no one would hear it.

I didn't bother calling Fatima before I popped up, but I knew that she was home because I could see the lights on in her kitchen. Jogging up the steps to her front porch, I banged on her door and rang the doorbell twice.

Seconds later, a nigga swung the door open, looking like he wanted to duke it out. "Yo, who da fuck is out here bangin'—"

I snatched my gun out and shoved it in his face before he could finish asking his question. "Nigga, you got three seconds to get the fuck on before I send these hollows at you!" I threatened.

He didn't trouble himself with putting his clothes on as he hightailed it to his car and peeled off. "Brian?!" Fatima called out from the kitchen. "Brian, who is it?!"

I quietly closed the door behind me and crept through her home with my hand on my heater.

"Bri—" Fatima froze in mid-sentence when she saw me standing in the entryway of her kitchen.

"F—Flex?!" she stuttered.

I gave her a devilish grin. "Don't act so surprised to see a nigga..."

"Where's Brian? What did you do to him?" she asked through clenched teeth.

"You oughta be more concerned with what I'm finna do to you," I said, slowly approaching her.

Fatima looked at the gun in my hand and tensed up. She had outed me before I was ready to be outed and I couldn't just forgive her for that shit.

"You ain't think I was gon' come see 'bout you, after that lil' stunt you pulled?"

"Flex, I—"

"Bitch, the whole hood is clownin' me now! Do you have any idea how that shit feels?! To be humiliated and ridiculed?!"

"Flex, baby, of course I do." She softly touched the side of my face. "I'm trans, remember?"

I jammed the barrel of my gun into her torso, but she didn't look as scared as she should've and that pissed me off even more.

"Fuck what those niggas think. If they can't accept you for who you are, then they never belonged in your life anyway," she said.

Suddenly, my grip on the gun loosened.

"Fuck the labels. Fuck your boys. And fuck Zuri," she said before kissing me.

Snatching away from her, I quickly unbuttoned my jeans and forced her head down to my waist. Fatima wasted no time giving me the blowjob of a lifetime. I had just started getting into it when my phone started ringing.

"*GAWK! GAWK!*" Fatima was making all sorts of slurping and gagging sounds as she passionately sucked me off. I forced it all the way down her throat till she got teary-eyed from the effort it took her to suck me. "*GAWK! GAWK! GAWK!*" There were tears coming out of her eyes and the whole nine. That bitch was really going in.

Placing my burner on the kitchen counter, I pulled out my phone and looked at the screen. It was Tommie calling me and I pretty much knew the reason he was reaching out. "What can I do for you, Boss Man?" I answered.

"Hmm. Let's see...you can start by telling me why Zuri and Rebel are still breathing!" he shouted into the receiver.

"*GAWK! GAWK!*" Fatima continued to deepthroat me and it took everything in me to keep from moaning in Tommie's ear as she did her thing.

"Don't worry, I'm on it," I told him.

After I hung up, I shot my seed down Fatima's throat. She looked up at me and smiled, like shit was all good. Then, I placed my gun to her temple and pulled the trigger.

POW!

Blood splattered onto the kitchen tile and her body hit the

floor with a hard thud. She might've just given me the best BJ of my life. But she had also humiliated the fuck out of me, and humiliation was a powerful emotion—one that could drive people to do things they'd never consider under normal circumstances. In a weird way, I also blamed Fatima for my father's death.

After leaving Fatima dead in a puddle of her own blood, I left her house as quickly as I'd cum in her mouth. On my way back to my car, I thought about Zuri and how I'd have to handle her, as well—eventually.

Truth be told, I hadn't put much thought into how I would kill her—or if I would even go through with it. My father's death had really taken its toll on me. I couldn't focus on shit else. Besides, I didn't think I was capable of killing the only person I'd ever loved romantically. So I had been stalling on offing her. But I knew if I didn't kill Zuri soon, Tommie would put me six feet under without a second thought.

15

ZURI

"So...how do you feel? You been experiencing any morning sickness?" I asked Sky as we walked down Sunset Boulevard. She was almost two months pregnant with Rebel's baby and the nigga had seemingly fallen off the face of the Earth. What were the odds of that happening, and right when she needed him most?

In an attempt to forget about our problems, we made plans to see a show at *The Comedy Store,* but it didn't start for another hour so we decided to take a stroll down the boulevard in the meantime. We'd been spending a considerable amount of time together lately, and it was almost like our fight in Tommie's office had never happened. We had somehow restored our alliance.

"A little," Sky said. "But not really. Not as much as I experienced when I was pregnant with Chosen," she added.

"Speaking of Chosen, how's my lil' boyfriend doing?" I asked her.

"He's good. Happy to be back in school. He couldn't wait to tell the other kids how he survived a mass shooting." Sky smirked and shook her head. "That's what he calls it, girl. A mass shooting."

We both laughed at that one.

"I don't have the heart to tell him what a mass shooting really is," she said. "He told me all the kids think he's cool now. And that they don't make fun of him for wearing hearing aids anymore."

"Well, that's what's up." I smiled. "I'm glad they decided to chill, cuz bitch, I fights kids too," I teased. "Ain't nobody gon' talk shit about my lil' boyfriend and get away with it!"

Sky started laughing even harder.

"So...how is Haven handling the news?" I asked, taking on a serious tone.

"The news?" Sky repeated, confused. "Oh...you mean the baby." She sighed deeply, then ran a hand through her naturally long hair. She had a small pudge but she wasn't showing significantly. But if you took one look at her you could definitely tell that she was preggers!

"He's not happy about it. But he's not forcing me to get an abortion or anything like that either," she said. "Not that I would abort my baby anyway," she added hastily. "As a matter of fact, he told me that he wants to raise the baby as his own...granted, I never see or talk to Rebel again," she added surreptitiously.

I shook my head at the pettiness of her baby father. Haven never ceased to amaze me. "*Mmm, mmm, mmm*. The highs and lows of motherhood," I said. "Too bad I'll never get to experience it...unless me and Flex adopt. And I doubt he'll ever be down for that. Flex is just not about that life," I admitted.

There was a long, tense silence between us before Sky spoke again.

"So, is it really true...about what you said in the club? You really are a...?" Her voice trailed off like she was scared to say the word 'transwoman'.

"Trans?" I finished for her. We hadn't talked about it since that night.

Sky sheepishly nodded her head.

"Yeah. It's true," I answered.

"Why didn't you tell me this shit sooner, Z? You're my girl. Hell, you're like a sister to me. I wouldn't have judged you," she stressed. "Back in the club, I never meant to offend you. On God, I wasn't trying to disrespect or degrade you in any way. I love and respect the fuck out of you! I was just shocked! If I had told you that shit, wouldn't you have been just as surprised?"

I nodded. "That's understandable," I said. "Perhaps I was a bit *too* defensive. Talking about my past life has never been easy for me. I just want to be accepted for who I am now."

"And I do accept you." Sky wrapped her arm around my shoulder and hugged me as we walked.

"You know...with everything that's been happening, I never got a chance to apologize to you. What I did to you back in Tommie's office...that shit was fucked up...and I'm really sorry, Sky."

"It was fucked up," she agreed. "But it's okay. I'll forgive you this one time," she grinned. "But don't let that shit happen again or I'm going upside your head, bitch," she warned.

That was understandable too. "And you'd have every right to," I laughed. "So, you still haven't heard from Rebel?" I asked her, slyly changing the subject.

Sky looked down at the ground. "Nope."

"Damn," I sighed.

Sky shrugged. "Fuck it... Life goes on," she said, pretending to be unaffected by his sudden absence. But I knew her ass better than she knew herself. She was hurting. Her heart probably ached every time she thought about Rebel.

"Right now, I'm just focusing on finding a new job. I've got three mouths to feed including the one in my belly. Plus, I have to pay Tommie back all the money I stole from him," she said.

"Haven just got out and he has hella felonies, so finding legit work hasn't been easy for him."

"Well, that bottle girl shit is out of the question. Tommie put the word out and now no clubs will hire us. We're better off getting a normal nine-to-five. Maybe I could ask Flex if he can help Haven find some work."

"Sorry, sis, but I don't think I want my baby daddy involved in the shit Flex be into."

Before I could argue with Sky's logic, a guy called out to me from behind. "Aye! Mamí in the pink dress!"

Me and Sky both turned around and saw Sintana jogging over toward us. I immediately recognized him from Club Allure. He came up there all the time and he was cool with all the local rappers, like YG and The Game. He was an up-and coming-artist himself, but he had yet to make waves. No one outside of LA knew his corny ass.

"Wassup wit' it?" he said once he reached me.

I gave him a flirty smile. "You tell me."

Sin licked his lips. "Shit, you married? I'm sure a nigga got you on lockdown, as fine as you are."

This was his first time ever trying to holla at me, and I couldn't help but wonder if he'd keep that same energy once he found out I was trans.

"Look, Sin. We don't want no trouble, okay?" Sky cut in. She had never liked him for whatever reason. Then again, Sky didn't like plenty of people for no reason at all. She had bullied poor Jessica for several weeks prior to us being fired.

"No disrespect, shorty, but I'm talkin' to yo girl right now," he said calmly. "You old news. And if she ain't want trouble, she wouldn't be walkin' 'round in this tight ass dress," he said, biting his lip.

I had never cheated on Flex. Never even seriously enter-tained the thought of it. But as I stood in front of this wanna-be ass rapper, I found myself debating on if I wanted to. At the very least, I could use him to make my man jealous. Flex's attention had been on everyone and everything else *but* me. Sure, Tommie kept him tied down but shit just wasn't like it used to be between us and I'd give anything to get that old thing back.

"Why don't you give me your number? Maybe we can get into some trouble together," I proposed.

Sky shot me a look that said 'I wouldn't do that'.

"A'ight, bet," Sin said, all giddy like a kid on Christmas.

Little did I know, I was taking on far more trouble than I could handle.

16

REBEL

Cruising down the boulevard with the heater in my lap, I looked for Tommie or anyone affiliated with him. I'd gone to their spas to look for them but they hadn't shown up since my return. I even stopped by Club Allure a couple times, but Tommie hadn't made an appearance in ages. He'd even appointed an assistant manager to handle his managerial duties while on leave. If I didn't know any better, I'd think Tommie was purposely ducking me 'cuz he knew a nigga wanted smoke.

Suddenly, out of nowhere, I spotted Sky and Zuri walking into *The Comedy Store*. A pretty face that would turn heads more than once was hard to miss. She stood out. Even in the middle of a busy place.

I caught a brief glimpse of her slightly protruding belly and I knew, without a shadow of a doubt, she was pregnant.

"Damn..."

A mixture of emotions hit me at once and it took me several seconds to realize the seriousness of the situation. If I hadn't seen her now, how long would it have been until I found out she was knocked up? How much time would've progressed?

"Damn, damn, damn," I cursed under my breath. I felt like I was dreaming.

I was so shocked when I saw her that I almost crashed into the parked car in front of me. Sky had all of my attention—she had never lost it. I didn't even notice that the light had turned red because I was too busy looking at her. That's how fucked up I was from seeing her stomach. Not to mention I had a half a gram of coke in my system, so I was processing the news a lot differently than I would sober. A nigga hadn't been the same ever since that fateful night and I couldn't wait to give Tommie's ass the entire clip.

Placing the burner in my dashboard, I made a swift U-turn and headed towards *The Comedy Store*, nearly causing a collision due to my impulsiveness. I had to see Sky and talk to her. I had to know if that baby she was carrying was mine or Blade's. We were both fucking with her around the same time so there was really no telling.

I thought about reaching out to her sooner, but it seemed unfair to her to try to pursue something that neither of us were ready for. I still hadn't gotten over my father's death and Sky still hadn't gotten over her baby daddy.

I could just see it in her eyes the day of our ice cream date. She still loved the nigga, and at this low point in my life, I was in no place to compete for her heart, so I just fell back. It was the only logical thing I could think to do to keep the peace between us. Besides, I didn't wanna endanger her or her son, especially now that Tommie was out here looking to put me in a box. Knowing him, he had probably put a bounty on my head and everything, and I didn't want Sky or Chosen caught in the crosshairs because of our feud. It had nothing to do with them and I cared about them too damn much to jeopardize their safety.

"Damn... I gotta talk to shorty, regardless," I convinced myself. "I gotta know for sure." I couldn't stay away knowing there was a possibility that she was carrying my seed. What type of nigga would I be if I ran away from my responsibilities?

By the time I finally found a parking space, Sky and Zuri were already inside the venue. I would've felt like an asshole if I went in and forced her to come outside and talk to me, so I stood at the outdoor bar and waited for the show to end. In order to kill time, I had a few shots to ease my stress.

Two hours later, Sky and Zuri finally walked out with the rest of the patrons, still laughing from the set. The shit must've been funny as fuck. Suddenly, I regretted not buying a ticket. I hadn't laughed in ages.

"Sky!" I called out.

As soon as her eyes locked on me, her mouth fell open in shock. "Rebel?"

Even Zuri looked surprised to see me. It was almost like they thought I was dead or some shit. Maybe they did after the way I had ghosted her.

"Wassup, my heart... I need to holla at you," I slurred, stumbling over towards her. I was drunk and high, and I accidentally came off aggressive as fuck. Grabbing her roughly by the arm, I dragged her over to the side of the building to talk in private.

"Aye, bruh. Be easy," the security guard warned me. He didn't appreciate what looked like me manhandling a woman.

"Man, this shit ain't got shit to do wit'chu," I said. "Fall back."

"Aye, you know this nigga?" the security guard asked Sky. He looked ready to fuck me up if she said no. And honestly, I was in no condition to fight with my fucked-up leg so I prayed she didn't say that... For his sake. I still had the burner on me.

Sky looked me up and down in confusion, then snatched her arm away. "I thought I did..."

The security guard mean-mugged me, and I had to hold back from blazing his ass up.

"Sky..." I gazed at her tenderly. "I just wanna talk...that's all," I slurred. I was weak because of the strong attraction I felt towards her, more so after I realized that I loved her.

Sky shook her head. "You had over a month to do that," she said in an angry tone. "I didn't know what the fuck had happened to you. I didn't know if you were dead or alive... I was worried sick!" Tears came to her eyes as she let me have it. "Now you wanna pop up on me, drunk as fuck, and expect to have a conversation—like shit's all good? You couldn't even pick up the fucking phone and call me!"

I had to fight to not to reach out and hold her. "Sky, let me explain—"

"I don't wanna hear shit you gotta say, Rebel," she said, walking around me.

"Sky!" I tried to go after her but the security guard thwarted my path.

"You heard the lady. Fall back," he said, parroting my own words at me.

I wanted to crack him in his shit, but I knew that wouldn't solve my problems. If anything, it would only make shit worse for me.

Zuri walked past me and rolled her eyes. "You foul as fuck, Rebel," she said. "You could've at least called Sky. She was driving herself crazy about your ass."

Hearing that shit made me feel bad. "Zuri, you don't understand—"

"Oh, I understand," she argued. "I understand that you're no different than the rest of these no-good niggas." She started to leave, then stopped in her tracks suddenly. "By the way, I heard what happened and I'm sorry about your folks. But that don't make what you did to Sky justifiable. You still ain't shit," she added in a cynical tone.

Her insult was a sharp blow to my pride.

Ignoring her comment, I called out to Sky again. "Aye, my heart! At least tell me if it's mine..."

Sky stopped in her tracks and turned around. "I'm not your baby. And neither is the one in my stomach," she spat.

The comment and its implication instantly made me sick to my stomach. My jaw tensed in anger. "So, it's Blade's?" I asked heatedly. I wanted to find that hoe ass nigga and put him in the ground just because. I still owed him an ass whooping for that fuck boy shit he pulled on Sky. What type of nigga robbed his own bitch?

Instead of answering, Sky walked off with Zuri, leaving me in suspense.

My throat was dry from the bitter taste left in my mouth. I was sick as fuck after hearing that shit.

Damn... So Blade is the father after all, I concluded. I felt like I was dreaming. I couldn't think straight.

Now that I knew the truth, I really felt like shit.

17

HAVEN

I was riding 'round the hood, strapped to the teeth as I searched for Blade like a bounty hunter looking for a wanted criminal. I knew his pussy ass was behind that hit. It didn't take rocket science to figure that shit out.

I hadn't made any enemies behind bars. I kept to myself and I kept my nose clean for the most part, and there was only one nigga I had beef with on the outs. My younger cousin, who'd gotten a lil' beside himself these days.

The nigga had been gunning for my spot ever since I got locked up. At first, I thought he just admired me and looked up to me. But now, I knew for certain that he'd always wanted my life—even before the judge threw the book at me. The nigga must've felt guilty about it because he'd been keeping in touch and supporting me throughout my prison stint. He had also been fucking my baby mama but that was neither here nor there.

Anyway, I promised that nigga I'd do him dirty when I got out but I honestly had no intentions of killing his ass. I just wanted to pump a lil' fear in his heart, so I paid some young niggas to beat his ass. I wasn't really going to murder my own peoples. I just wanted to teach his bitch ass a lesson. But the nigga was obviously left shook after that whole ordeal. So shook that he felt the need to retaliate. He drew first blood, but I was gonna give that nigga a war he wouldn't believe. He'd put my son in the hospital. I couldn't let that shit ride.

I didn't bother telling Sky that Blade was the one who'd shot at us because I knew she would try to stop me from killing him. And I didn't wanna hear her fucking mouth about the matter. Besides, I was gonna do me regardless.

After coming up empty-handed, I headed back to Glendale where my baby mama lived. Blade was keeping a low profile to avoid confrontation and not attract any attention to himself. Back in the day, you could always catch him on the block but he was moving smarter now.

Sintana had texted me a couple days ago, saying he saw Blade up at Club Allure, talking to the owner. But he claimed the nigga came with a dozen niggas and that they all looked like they weren't playing any games. I didn't give a fuck about all that, though. I had enough ammunition to blow their whole camp down and I still pulled up. But by the time I got there, he and his entourage were already gone. Luck was clearly on his side.

The nigga was moving like a mobster now. I knew it wouldn't be easy to get at him, but it was still possible, none-theless. That nigga might've kept them shooters with him now that he knew I was looking for him, but he wasn't untouchable. He could still get this action.

I finally made it back to my crib and saw that Sky's BMW was parked in her designated space. She was home after running the streets with Zuri and I could only imagine the trouble those two had gotten into. Zuri had always been a bad influence on my girl and I wasn't all surprised to learn that she'd dragged Sky into her underworld of scams. I had never really liked Zuri but Sky was a grown ass woman, who was fully capable of making her own friends and her own decisions in life.

As soon as I walked in the crib, I found Sky in the living room, sitting on the sofa and staring at the blank TV in front of her. She seemed to be lost in thought. She didn't even address me when I walked in.

"Fuck is up with you?" I asked her.

"Nothing," she lied, snapping out of her brief reverie.

"You look pissed about somethin'. Did anything happen while you were out?"

"I'm not pissed, Haven," she said in an exasperated tone. "I'm just tired, that's all."

"Good." I closed and locked the door behind me. "I was finna say, you've got no reason to be pissed anyway."

Sky glared at me. "What's that supposed to mean?"

"I mean, I'm sayin'...it ain't like I went out and knocked up some bitch."

"Haven, do not start," Sky warned me.

"Trust me, I haven't even begun to tell you how I really feel about the shit!" I'd been biting my tongue since the welcome home party, but I couldn't hold back anymore. I had to let that bitch know how I felt.

"Nigga, you're acting like I cheated on you or some shit. We weren't even together."

"Bitch, it don't matter! You betrayed my trust!" I hollered.

"How?!"

"Fuck you mean how? By fuckin' my cousin!"

"How was I supposed to know that Blade was your cousin?! You never told me that shit!"

"I shouldn't have to! You were supposed to hold it down while I was locked up! Not sleep with every nigga you came in contact with! I should knock yo fuckin' top off for that shit!"

Sky jumped to her feet. "Nigga, you married a whole bitch! You don't see me giving you shit about that!"

"Yeah, and I took care of that," I argued. "That shit is over and done with. But you..." I paused and shook my head at her. "Sky... This is somethin' we have to deal with for eighteen years," I told her.

I had already committed myself to helping her raise the kid. I loved the idea of us being a family, regardless of her baby not being mine. I was happy to be part of my son's life again. Now that we were reunited, I couldn't take a chance on losing them again. I'd lose my freedom before I lost my family.

"Haven, nobody is begging you to help raise this baby. And being a parent doesn't just stop after eighteen years. You are more than welcome to leave now if you want to," Sky said with a dismissive wave of her hand.

I almost wanted to break that bitch. "And let Blade raise my kid?! Hell nah!" I spat. He'd been playing house with my family for far too long.

"Would you stop saying that shit?! FOR GOD'S SAKE, THIS AIN'T BLADE'S BABY!!!" Sky shouted at the top of her lungs.

"What?" I slowly approached her with clenched fists. "Fuck you mean that ain't Blade's baby?!" I pointed at her belly.

"I didn't get pregnant by him," she whispered, looking down at her feet.

I snatched her up by her arm and shook her violently, damn near snapping her shit in half. "Then who the fuck knocked you up?!" I screamed. "JUST HOW MANY NIGGAS DID YOU FUCK WHILE I WAS GONE?!"

"Let go of me, Haven! You're hurting me!" she cried.

I finally released her. "Nah, bitch... *You* hurtin' *me*," I said before storming out of the apartment. I couldn't stand to look at Sky a second longer because she was this close to getting her grill knocked out.

18

SKY

After Haven stormed out of my crib like the little bitch he was, I went to pick up Chosen from Leilani's place. I was supposed to pick him up after the show, but I needed a brief moment of solitude to collect myself. That heated interaction with Rebel took a lot out of me. Here it was, I thought the nigga was dead. But instead, he was just avoiding me. Then he had the nerve to think I actually wanted to talk to his ass.

Regardless of what happened to his family, I was tired of him playing mind games with me. I wasn't the one who massacred his loved ones. I wasn't the one who popped back up in his life after 16 years and made him fall in love with me. I was innocent in all of this shit—but Rebel insisted on treating me like I was responsible for everything that went wrong in his life. He made shit this way when it didn't have to be like this. And it was sad too because I wanted to be there for him during his time of need—but not if it would only leave me broken-hearted in the end.

Rebel had already shown me that he was inconsistent as fuck. If I opened my heart to him again, there was a huge possibility that he would leave it shattered to pieces. I was better off without his sometimey ass. I wasn't here for that back-and-forth shit. Not to mention, I was still trying to make it work with my baby daddy. Speaking of my baby daddy, I wasn't sure where he had run his ass off to—and to be frank, I didn't care. I needed some time away from him. He could really be a handful at times.

After picking up Chosen, I drove back home and ran him a warm bath once we got inside. "Mommy, can Daddy make us dinner on the beach like Rebel?" my son asked as he played with his action figures in the bathtub.

He was in a talkative mood after leaving my cousin's home. She pretty much let him do whatever he wanted. We all had him spoiled senseless.

I gently scrubbed his back and sighed. "Daddy is still trying to find a job," I told him using ASL.

"Why?"

"Baby, I told you," I began in a calm tone. "Daddy just got out of prison..."

What's prison, Chosen signed.

A place that bad men go to for doing bad things, I signed back.

"Daddy is a bad man?" Chosen asked in an unnaturally high-pitched tone. Because he was deaf, he couldn't hear what he sounded like when he spoke and that sometimes made it difficult for others to interpret. Usually, he only talked around people he was comfortable with. He always spoke around Rebel though.

"Not anymore," I told him.

"Is Rebel a bad man?" he asked next.

I looked down at the water and thought about Rebel, and the love I had for him that would never go away. "C'mon, little one. Let's get you rinsed off and ready for bed," I said, ignoring his question.

After drying him off, I helped him put his PJs on and said

prayers with him before tucking him in. Moscow, our senior Russian Blue, leapt onto his mattress and snuggled close. He and Chosen were best friends.

I had just leaned down to kiss him goodnight when he suddenly asked me something I wasn't prepared to answer. "Mommy, are you mad at Rebel?"

Moscow lifted his head and stared at me with emerald green eyes, almost like he was waiting to hear my response as well.

"Sweet dreams, little one," I said, kissing him on the forehead. I didn't have the heart to tell him yes.

I stood to my feet and quietly closed the door behind me, and not even two seconds later, there was a knock on the front door.

"Haven's dumb ass must've forgot his keys," I told myself.

Stomping to the door, I swung it open without looking through the peephole first. To my surprise, it wasn't Haven standing there. It was the last person I expected to see and I was tempted to slam the door in his fucking face.

"Why the hell are you here, Rebel?" I asked, unenthused.

He smiled and shook his head at me, and my heart did a silly, little flutter. The proximity created a charged moment between us, and we gazed at one another for what felt like an eternity in silence.

Suddenly, he surprised me when he leaned in towards my face. His lips touched mine and it was the single greatest feeling in the world. The warm, wet sensation of his kiss penetrated through my very being.

My eyes shut and I crumbled underneath the pressure of his touch and before I knew it my lips had parted and his tongue had moved inside my mouth, toying and flicking with my own. All inhibitions about letting go evaporated into thin air. In that moment, I just surrendered to him, enraptured in an ever-growing torrid kiss.

"*Mmm*," I mumbled softly as his lips roamed from my lips to my ear. I gasped when his tongue found its way in. He devoured my flesh like it was dessert and I gave myself to him. "Rebel..." I tried to move away, but he grabbed me by the waist and held me tight, his enticing scent washing over me.

"Don't run from me, baby. Don't push me away," he whispered against my mouth. "You da one who made me like this. So take some damn responsibility."

My lips quivered and I hesitated for a moment. The feel of his bare skin and the comforting sound of his heartbeat made me feel at ease. Like I was finally home and my pussy ached in anticipation.

"Rebel," I moaned as he kissed the side of my neck. My breasts pushed against his chest. He was making it so damn hard for me to hold back. I was in the worst mood after my fight with Haven, but one touch from Rebel was enough to calm me down.

Sliding my hands up his chest, I wrapped them around his neck and he pulled me into him and I melted against his strong, thick body.

He cupped my chin. "You really drive me fuckin' crazy," he confessed. "It makes it so damn hard for me to think straight. So forgive me if I don't always make the right calls."

"Why did you stay away for as long as you did?" I asked him as his fingers trailed along my back.

"Sky...you mean more to me than anything else in this world. I only stayed away 'cuz I thought it was the right thing to do," he revealed.

I mean-mugged his ass, then he kissed the glare right off my face and I just melted into him. My annoyance disappeared in a blaze of lust. I had missed him so damn much and it made it hard for me to stay mad. My mind was filled with only him. It seemed like it was only when people were gone that you noticed their presence in your life.

"I tried, baby. Lord knows I tried, but I don't think I can live without you," he told me. "Fate's screaming at me that this is meant to be and I ain't 'bout to fuck with fate." He kissed me again and held me tighter in his arms. "I don't care that you carrying that nigga's seed... I want all of this to be mine forever."

Without words, I hopped up onto him and wrapped my legs around his waist. The line I had carefully drawn between him and I became invisible. My mind was yelling at me to stop, but my body was saying a completely different thing. I knew that he was married, but I still wanted to feel him deep inside me. Once again, my heart and body were contradicting each other.

I'd been missing him like crazy. The way he felt when I touched him. His expressions. His scent. Everything about him. No matter how much he'd crushed my heart, I simply couldn't forget about him. He was my hope, my light, my everlasting shelter.

Rebel carried me to my room and gently placed me down onto the mattress like I was made of porcelain. He undressed himself, then freed me of my clothes next. My gaze dropped to his very obvious—and very large—erection. I licked my lips when I saw a pearl of precum appear on the head of his giant dick.

Reaching up, I grabbed his rock-hard dick and guided it towards my pussy. Even I was shocked to discover how wet I was down there. With a seductive smile on my face, I rubbed the tip against my throbbing clit and shivered at the sensation.

"Open up for me, my heart," he urged, maintaining a slow, insistent pressure until my body opened and he slid partially inside.

Desperate for more of that overwhelming stretch, I lifted my hips again and gained another inch. A tiny groan escaped his lips as he slid between my folds. I wanted him bad as fuck and I didn't care about the consequences!

Inch by inch, he slid in with ease and stopped long enough just to savor his penetration. His dick twitched a little inside of me and his jaw tensed in appreciation. I hadn't been fucked since that night and my body craved him to no end.

Rebel slid into me a little deeper and I arched my back to accept all of him as wave after wave of pleasure moved through me. His dick was so long that he filled me up in an instant. I barely had a chance to adjust to his size before he was hammering into me, making my head hit the button tufted headboard.

"Sky...?"

My nipples were diamond hard and he leaned down and sucked each of them.

"Yeah, baby?" I cooed.

"How this shit feel?" he asked.

I ran my fingers through his locs, admiring his tattoos, full lips, and sultry eyes. "*Mmm—ooohhh—unhhh,*" I moaned incoherent words and he smiled at me sympathetically.

"That good, huh?" he teased, filling me up with long, slow strokes. "Don't hold back now, baby. Let me hear it."

I tried to say something, but the euphoric feeling he gave me had rendered me speechless. He pounded into my body with rough strokes that made my nails dig harder into his shoulders. It was like he was pulling the orgasm out of me, demanding that my body obey him.

"You feel me fuckin' the shit outta you," he whispered against my lips. "I'm inside you, baby. Deep inside this wet ass pussy. Tell a nigga how it feels. I need to hear it..."

"Fuck it feels so good," I moaned.

Suddenly, I realized that what we were doing was wrong, and in spite of him feeling so damn good in me, I begged him to pull out.

Rebel didn't listen as he continued to jackhammer me into oblivion, occasionally rotating his hips in a circular motion.

Ignoring my higher self, I started moving my hips up and down, meeting his every thrust.

Looking up from our conjoined sexes, I noticed his aroused expression and that he appeared to be concentrating hard as fuck.

"Rebel," I begged. "Pleeeeaaassseee," I whined. "Pull out!" I demanded, even though he was hitting my shit right.

My pleas went unheeded and Rebel continued to pump back and forth. "You suckin' me in so hard, it's hard to pull out," he groaned. "This shit is tight as fuck, Sky."

He kissed me again and I clung to his broad shoulders as the kiss intensified. "Rebel," I whimpered. My cheeks flushed and my body became hot as I flooded his dick with juices. My legs shook wildly and I began to orgasm. I had never cum so hard in all my life! "Oh, fuck," I moaned, voice trembling with passion.

There was sudden jolt of electricity that shot through me as my body convulsed. I cried out into his mouth as he kept kissing me.

I quickly pulled back. "Stop!" I squealed as my legs shook uncontrollably. He was still plowing into me, despite making me cum a second ago. And I was still just as wet as ever. "Please, Rebel...stop," I pleaded as tears of pleasure poured down my cheeks. He was hitting my G-spot unmercifully.

"Why, when this shit is all soft and wet?" he moaned, plunging in me until he hit rock bottom.

He moved his hands to the small of my back and held me in place as he drilled me in short, rapid bursts.

"Rebel!" I cried out his name, coming close to my peak again. I squeezed my eyes shut as I accepted the powerful, approaching orgasm.

"Open your eyes... Look at me, baby," he whispered.

I opened my eyes and looked up at his beautiful, chocolate face.

"The way you lookin' at me now... Don't look at no other nigga like that," he said.

"Okay, baby," I whined. There was just so much of him, all of it big and black and hard.

He leaned down and kissed me. "Whose is it?" he growled, fucking me harder, faster and deeper.

"It's yours!" I bellowed. "I'm yours! The baby's yours!"

"The baby's mine?" he asked, tapping my G-spot repeatedly.

I was cumming and gushing everywhere! "Yesssss!!!" I cried out. I was going crazy because it felt so good.

My hands came from around his neck and grabbed his shoulders, my nails digging in as I rocked my hips more and more. I felt his dick jerk in me and I knew he was close to cumming as well.

"This time...I won't let you go," he said.

Rebel slammed into me again and again, and my head fell back as a low stuttering moaning wail came from my throat and I convulsed in a sweet, mind-blowing orgasm of delight.

"Fuuucccckk!" he groaned before spilling his seeds into me.

My breathing slowed after a couple of minutes, but my pussy muscles were still contracting. He gripped my hips and kissed me deep and slow as I continued to twitch and tremble from my orgasm. My grip on his shoulders became weak and he quickly shifted his hands up behind my back to support me.

"I love you, Sky," he whispered before kissing me.

"I love you, too. But I'm still mad at your ass."

Despite cumming, Rebel didn't pull out just yet. He was still buried to the hilt in me, which was intensely erotic to say the least.

There was a dreamy smile on his face as he looked down at me. For a married man, he didn't look as guilty as he should've. However, I felt guilty as fuck!

"We shouldn't have done this shit again," I panted, staring up at the ceiling. "What about your wife?"

He pinched my chin lightly. "Ex-wife," he corrected me.

I immediately propped my head up on my elbow and glared at him. "You got a divorce?"

Rebel nodded his head. "Yeah...and the shit was long overdue," he added.

"Is that why you stayed away for as long as you did? You needed time to get over her?" I asked him.

He scoffed and shook his head. "Is that what you think?"

"I don't know what to think anymore. You're hard to read. And you're always ghosting my ass."

Rebel grabbed my hand and kissed the back of it. "I promise not to ghost you again."

"You've made a lot of promises that you didn't keep," I reminded him. "Shit is just too shaky with you. I'm not sure I can ever place my faith into the hands of a man like that."

His eyes slightly flared with anger. "So what'chu sayin'?" he asked, offended.

"I'm saying the sex was nice...but I wanna make shit work with my baby daddy." I had to get my senses back, now that we'd gotten that out of our system.

His eyebrows pointed up in an inquisitive fashion. "But you just told me the baby was mine."

I averted my eyes to prevent anymore awkwardness. "That doesn't mean I want you to be a part of its life. Rebel, you made your choice. So now, I have to make mine."

He was taken aback, and it took him a few seconds to recover. "Wow..." Rebel shook his head in disappointment, then slowly climbed out of the bed and put his clothes back on. "I cannot believe what the fuck I'm hearin' right now."

I didn't say anything as I watched him walk toward the door. Suddenly, he stopped dead in his tracks and turned to face me.

"I love the fuck outta you, Sky... You're the biggest part of my life," he stressed. "From the very first moment I saw you as a kid, I knew that you were my soulmate. You're the best thing to ever happen to me," he said, his voice tender and warm. "Look, I'm sorry that I made you feel like you can't trust me. That's the last thing a nigga wanna do... But if this baby really is mine, Sky... I can't just walk away from that shit. And I can't just walk away from you."

I had really lost my senses. The bastard had completely bewitched me. Climbing out of bed, I walked over towards him and stood on my tiptoes to kiss him. My heart felt like it was about to burst. I was so confused. On one hand, I wanted to be with Rebel. But there was a part of me that felt obligated to make it work with my baby daddy. Our son was the thread that connected us.

Why did I have to be stuck in this dilemma?

Why couldn't I just make up my mind?

"I love you," I told him.

"I love you, too." He hugged me tight with his thick and tatted, powerful arms.

"I do wanna be with you, Rebel. But I don't have time for the games and BS. If you're going to be a part of my life, then I need you to stay solid."

He smiled sweetly at my scowl. "Baby, I wouldn't wanna be anything less," he assured me.

We kissed, his long tongue dueling with mine as he devoured me. Then, he pulled back to look me in the eyes.

"You sure about this, right?" he asked. "'Cuz I'm not letting you go, even if you change your mind."

Before I could answer, Haven walked into the bedroom with a loaded gun aimed right at our heads.

19

REBEL

Haven cocked an eyebrow questioningly. "Making plans without me, baby?" he asked Sky. "I'on know how to feel about that..." He shot me a prompt and piercing glare.

We were both surprised by his intrusion. We didn't even hear his ass come in the apartment. We were too busy wrapped up in our moment.

"Haven...what the fuck are you doing?" she asked through clenched teeth. "Why the hell do you have a gun?"

I immediately stepped in front of her to shield her body with my own. As her man and best friend, I would protect her at any and all costs. Just like I used to as a boy.

"Nah, the real question is, what the fuck are *you* doing?" he countered. "A nigga ain't even been gone two hours and you already givin' my pussy to some sucka nigga. I should blow a hole through yo skull just because! Fuck you think this is?!" he growled.

"Put that fucking gun down, Haven!" Sky screamed. "Before you wake up our son!"

His dark eyes held me in a steady gaze as he spoke to Sky.

"*Is* he our son?" Haven asked Sky in a doubtful tone. "'Cuz at the rate you been goin', it really ain't no tellin'."

Sky glared at him and he cocked the hammer to his gun as he kept it aimed at my head.

"Nigga, you should'a been got blazed. I let you live for the simple fact that you were no longer a threat to me," he explained. "But here you are, standing in my house, next to my bitch, violating me and everything I stand for. I got every right to knock you out'cho fuckin' clothes."

"Haven—"

"Shut the fuck up, Sky! Yo ass done said—and did enough!" Haven snapped at her.

"Look, bruh, I'm askin' you nicely," I began. "Put the fuckin' burner away. Let's just dead all this shit and talk like men." I politely but firmly invited him to chill the fuck out. The lump in my throat expanded as I waited for him to make his move.

"Keep it all the way real," Haven said to Sky, ignoring me. "How long dis shit been goin' on since I been out?"

"Oh my God, Haven! You're acting fucking crazy! How do you expect me to talk to you with a gun to my head?! At least, put the gun away so we can have a mature, civil conversation."

"Keep it a thousand," he insisted. "You been fuckin' dis nigga since I came home, haven't you?"

Before she could answer, I rushed him and the gun went off, shattering the mirror on the dresser. Sky screamed as I tackled him to the floor and I managed to get the gun out of his hand before he used it on either of us.

It didn't take a lot to disarm his punk ass and he looked mad as fuck that I'd gotten the upper-hand so quickly. "Fuck off me!" he spat, kneeing me in the gut—where I'd been shot.

I groaned in pain and doubled over and he wasted no time wailing on me.

"Stop it, Haven! Get off of him!" Sky yelled, running to my rescue.

She pushed him and he backslapped the shit out of her.
WHAP!

Seeing him put his hands on her put me in a homicidal
state of mind, and I jumped to my feet and grabbed his ass and
slammed him onto his head. Before he could recover, I climbed
on top of him and started reigning blows all over his head and
chest.

"REBEL, STOP! YOU'RE GONNA KILL HIM!" Sky cried as
I beat his ass with every ounce of strength I had—which wasn't
much, considering my condition. Still, I was a fuckin' loose
cannon!

"That's the plan!" I shouted, a flood of icy rage sweeping
through me. I was blindsided by my own anger, off my crutches
and on one as I stole on his ass repeatedly. Someone had to feel
my wrath, since I had yet to take my frustrations out on
Tommie. Why not him? It wasn't like his ass didn't deserve the
shit. He'd just had a gun pointed at us a second ago.

I beat and punched him until he was bloody and disfigured.
"YOU'RE   GONNA   KILL   HIM!   STOOOPPPP!"   Sky
screamed.

She tried to pull me off of him, but I shoved her and kept on
punching him over and over until he was hardly conscious.
Blood sprayed everywhere and my knuckles were busted up. I
was just about to choke him until he stopped breathing when I
felt the cold, hard steel of a gun press into the back of my head.

"I told your ass to stop!" Sky said with a manic glint in her
eyes. She wasn't used to my murderous and animalistic
behavior and she looked like she was terrified of me.

I immediately froze in place, surprise and sorrow warring in
my heart.

*Did this bitch really just put a gun to my head? And right after I
poured my heart out to her ass?*

I crumbled as a small piece of me broke inside. I felt hurt
and betrayed. She obviously cared more about this sorry ass

nigga than she did me. Why else would she be pointing the gun at me instead of Haven?

Slowly and deliberately, I stood to my feet, chest heaving and fists still clenched.

"Damn, so it's like that?" I asked with a look of disappointment on my face. I wasn't expecting her to switch up on me so fast. What happened to staying solid?

"Yeah, it's just like that," she said with an intense, unwavering gaze. "I want you out of my fucking house! NOW!!! And take your fucking drugs with you too!" She reached down, picked up my small plastic bag of coke and threw it at me. "It fell out of your pocket during the scuffle," she told me.

My face flared with embarrassment as I stared at her with pained eyes. "Sky..." I quickly shoved it in my pockets. "It ain't what you think. I'm not an addict or no shit like that," I said in denial. "Look, you don't know what I'm goin' through after losing my dad—"

"Muthafucka, I lost both of my parents at fourteen!" she reminded me, voice laced with frustration. "Believe me, I feel your pain. But I would never put that shit into my body and I can't trust *anyone* that does. I especially can't have someone like that around my kid."

I gave her a heartfelt stare. I had carried a torch for her all this time—even promised her that we'd live in a house together in Malibu, somewhere off the coast when we were just kids. I just knew we were made for each other. I couldn't lose her now, not again. She was my best fucking friend; my warmth when I felt cold.

"Sky—"

"Get the fuck out of my house, Rebel! I'm done talking!"

Haven slowly came to, and I looked down at him in anger. It took everything in me to keep from kicking him in his fucking head. I hated his ass and I wholeheartedly blamed him for the way Sky was acting right now. Or maybe I was just too damn stubborn to take some accountability for my own actions.

My throat tightened to the point where it was difficult to speak. "But the baby—"

"You will never see this fucking baby, Rebel. I can guarantee you that!" she yelled. "Now get the fuck out my house—before you don't see your 29th birthday either!"

I always swore she would be the end of me.

"*Ugh*...Sky..." Haven struggled to speak through his pain.

"You can get the fuck out too, nigga!" she told him. "I want both of ya'll asses out of my house and out of my life!!!"

20

ZURI

Flex was out—doing only God knows what with who knows who—so I decided to hit up Sintana to see if he could come through. Flex's trifling ass had been cheating on me left and right, and I finally felt like it was time to have my own lil' sneaky link. Besides, I always thought Sintana was kinda cute, but I never made a move on him because he was supposedly fucking with Sky's cousin Leilani. I wasn't trying to step on anyone's toes so I stayed in my lane.

Anyway, I Facetimed Sintana and was surprised to see him answer so abruptly. "Wuz good, sweetness? I been waitin' on you to hit me."

"What's up? What are you into right now?" I asked him.

"Shit, I wish I was in you," he smiled.

Hearing him say that shit made my booty hole tingle. Sin's lil' ass was a freak, or at least that's what Leilani had told us. I couldn't help that my curiosity had gotten the best of me. That bitch shouldn't have been bragging about how big his dick was, and how skillfully he used his tongue. Now I wanted to experience it for myself.

"*Mmmhmm.* I'm sure we can make that happen," I said,

cutting to the chase. I'd never had sex with anyone else but Flex, and I wanted to see if I was staying with him simply because I didn't know that there was better dick out there.

"Shit, where you at?" he asked.

"At the crib. Blowing on this good chronic," I told him.

"Shoot me the addy. I'm tryin' to pull up. You drink?" he asked. "Shit, I got some Patron with me to compliment the chronic."

"Bring it," I told him. "And bring a box of Trojans while you at it."

Sin chuckled. "Say less."

"I'm finna text you my address," I told him.

"A'ight, bet. See you in a few."

I hung up the phone, sent him my addy, then hopped in the shower so I'd be squeaky clean by the time he arrived. As I waited for him to get here, I thought about how I'd tell him I was a transwoman, and I thought about what his reaction would be. Would he be angry? Would he feel misled? Flex was the only man who knew the truth about me. Hell, me and Sky had been friends for six years and she'd only recently found out I was born a man. What would Sin think?

Speaking of Sin, he texted me to let me know he was outside and I immediately got butterflies. I hadn't had to sit down and tell someone I was trans since me and Flex started dating back in high school. And even back then, it was one of the hardest things I'd ever had to do.

I was wearing a pink, satin kimono from Victoria's Secret when I opened the door for him smelling like coconut body butter. I hardly had a chance to greet the nigga before he grabbed me and started sticking his tongue all down my throat.

"Sin, wait," I giggled.

"Fuck am I waiting for?" he breathed, squeezing all on my ass.

"Wait...there's something I gotta tell you," I said, weakly pushing him off.

He pulled me closer to him and started nibbling on my ear. "What'chu gotta tell me, baby?" He was horny as fuck. Probably too horny to even care and I considered keeping my secret to myself and letting him find out on his own. But that seemed like a fucked up thing to do to someone.

"Sin...I'm a...I—I—" I started stuttering over my own words and Sin took the initiative to undo my robe. The thin, sheer material fell at my feet and he got an eyeful of my semi-hard dick. I hadn't taped it down and it stood proudly in front of me —all six inches of it. "Sin, I...I—I was just about to tell you—"

"Chill," he smiled. "It's all good." He reached out and wrapped his hand around my dick. "This ain't my first rodeo," he said before getting down onto his knees.

"Wait! I gotta ask you somethin' first..."

"Am I gay? Hell nah, I ain't gay," he quickly said in denial.

I closed my eyes and tried my best to keep my cool. "That's not what I was going to ask you," I said.

"Well, wassup?"

"Are you and Leilani still a thing? 'Cuz I kinda feel bad for doing this if ya'll are still together."

"What?" Sintana laughed. "We just friends," he said.

"Just friends?" I repeated for verification.

"Just friends," he assured me before lowering his mouth onto my dick.

AFTER FUCKING the shit out of each other, we laid in bed and smoked a Backwood without a moral care in the world. "That shit was incredible," I told him. "Habit-forming. Now I'mma want it all the time," I said, stroking his dick back to life.

"Baby, this dick yours now," he said. "You can have it as often as you want it."

Sin was just as gifted as Leilani had claimed he was. He fucked me in every position and ate my ass like it was his last meal. The nigga was a certified freak! After today, I knew I could never go back to only fucking Flex. Sin had me adick-ted!

I was just about to swallow his cock when I heard the front door being unlocked. "Shit! My nigga back!" I said, jumping out of the bed in a panic.

"You got a nigga?" Sin asked jealously.

"*Sshh*!" I hissed at him. "Yeah, I got a nigga. And if he finds you in here with me he gon' light both our asses up! Now where did you park?" I whispered.

"Across the street. Why?" he asked in a low tone.

"Thank God!" It would've been all bad if he'd parked in the driveway. Flex would've instantly known that something was amidst. "You gon' have to leave out the back door," I whispered. "Hurry, before he comes!"

"Aye, bae, where you at?" Flex called out. "I got somethin' for you."

"Coming! I'm just fixing my hair," I lied.

"Girl, I don't give a fuck about your hair. Get'cho ass out here," he demanded.

Sin hastily pulled on his clothes and I pushed him toward the door leading to the back patio, which was conveniently in the bedroom. I wouldn't have been surprised if Flex had used it for the exact same reason, knowing his trifling ass.

"Hurry, hurry!" I whispered.

Suddenly, Sin stopped in his tracks. "I ain't goin' nowhere till you promise I'mma see you again," he said. His ass was bull-shitting and if he didn't leave soon, we were both going to be exposed—and killed.

"I promise, I promise!" I quickly opened the door and pushed him out of my house.

I tried to close the door in his face, but he put his hand on it and stopped me.

"Where my kiss at?" he asked. The nigga must've wanted to die. This bussy had his ass trippin'.

Caving to his demand, I leaned in and gave him a quick peck on the lips.

"ZURI!" Flex hollered.

"Coming!" I shouted after quietly closing and locking the door behind me. Talk about a close call! Next time, we would have to get a room. My heart couldn't handle this much tension.

I walked out of the bedroom and met Flex in the living room, where he was surrounded with bags from Nordstrom's, Chanel, Prada, Fendi, and Louis Vuitton. Someone had taken a stroll down Rodeo Drive.

"What the fuck took you so long?" he asked me.

I tried to fix my unkempt hair. I was sweating like a pedophile in a playground. "I told you. I was trying to fix my hair." I looked down at all the bags. "Oh my God, baby!" I gasped. "You bought all of this for me?" I asked him, feeling like a kid on Christmas. The gifts just kept getting better and better.

Suddenly, I felt bad for fucking another nigga. I had wanted to get back at Flex for all the cheating and heartache, but getting even didn't seem to give me the fulfillment I was looking for. It had only made my body feel good for a little while. But now, I felt like shit.

"It ain't all for you," he snorted. "I had to cop some new shit for myself, as well," he teased.

"Oh, baby!" I ran over to him and rained kisses all over his face and neck. "Thank you, thank you, thank you! You're the best!"

"I know I am."

I kissed his lips and hugged him tight.

"I know I ain't always the nigga you want me to be," Flex

said. "But I promise you, from here on out, I'mma start being the nigga you need."

Now that we had established that, I told myself I'd never cheat on him again. Or at least, I would try not to. Little did I know, that was easier said than done.

THE NEXT DAY, I met up with Sky for brunch at *Ysabel*, a fancy and contemporary restaurant/cocktail lounge on North Fairfax. Now that we were both unemployed, it wasn't in either of our best interests to be eating at a place so expensive. But I guess you could say old habits die hard. We were used to living the high-life. And we both still owed Tommie a shit ton of money!

"Okay, sis. Come through with the Fendi fit," she said, admiring my brown Fendi logo dress.

"You like it? Flex bought it for me yesterday," I bragged, giving her a little twirl before I sat down. Sky had on a basic flower-patterned maxi dress. White retro, cat-eye sunglasses sat perched atop her head. There was a small cup of green olives in front of her.

"Damn... Flex done stepped his shit all the way up, I see!" Sky said, nodding her head in approval.

"That's a Fendi fact," I agreed.

"I think I'm starting to like him a lot more these days."

"Girl, he's really been showing some improvement. I don't find myself bitching at him half as much as I used to. He's really stepped up his game." I picked up the menu. "Anyway, have you ordered yet?" I didn't want to pin all the roses on Flex too soon. He had disappointed me in the past so many times.

"I ordered a pitcher of Sangria for you, but I'm still waiting on them to bring it out. It's crackin' so it's a lil' busier than usual. I haven't ordered the food yet, though."

Just then, our waiter came out and placed the pitcher and

wine glasses in front of us. He didn't realize Sky was pregnant because her belly was hidden underneath the tablecloth. We ordered our food and once he was gone, Sky began her thorough and unnecessary investigation of Flex's new occupation.

"So, I guess Flex is finding his footing with his new job, huh?" she asked, being nosey as fuck.

I poured myself a glass of Sangria and took a sip. "Uh, yeah," I answered, purposely being vague.

She gave me a look of mixed admiration and jealousy. "What does this new job entail anyway?" she asked next, a curious gleam in her eyes.

I repressed an eye roll. "He does security. Same as he's always been doing," I lied. She didn't need to know the details.

"Girl, bye. I've known you and Flex a long time and he's never made more than minimum wage *when* he could keep a job," she sassed.

I felt an unexpected degree of tension and I cut my eyes at her in anger. "Somebody sounds salty." I charged it to her hormones to keep from cussing her ass out.

"You know I am certainly not one to be salty... I just wanna make sure Flex ain't doing some shit that might put you in a fucked up situation later on down the line. The one with Tommie is bad enough..."

"Girl, I'm a grown ass woman. Can't nobody put me in a situation I don't wanna be in," I told her. "You just let me worry about Flex..."

"Look, I ain't mean shit by it, I'm just saying," she said in her defense.

"Well, you wouldn't be saying shit if it was Haven or Blade securing a bag. All of a sudden, you're feeling judgy since it's my nigga flossin' instead of yours!"

"Judgy? Bitch, ain't nobody judging you. I just know the risk that comes with being involved in that street shit. You know my baby daddy used to be that nigga," she reminded me.

"Yeah, *used* to be," I said in petty triumph.

Sky rolled her eyes at me. "Well, since Flex has stepped up his game, do you plan on throwing away Sin's number?"

"Why would I?" I asked, offended. Sky was a little too invested in my personal business. Sure, we were best friends but not everything needed to be shared—especially if it came with judgment.

"Um...because he's dating my cousin," Sky said, in a tone that made me feel like she was talking to a child or a dummy.

"I asked him if they were kickin' it and he told me they were just friends," I said, rushing to his defense. I was still dick dizzy after the way he'd fucked me. A bitch could tell me he was a serial killer, and I'd probably still give him some ass. That lil' nigga knew how to lay some wood.

"Bitch, you are a naïve fool if you believe that," Sky said, shaking her head. "Niggas don't know how to be just friends."

"Well, that's what he said and he gave me no reason not to believe him."

Sky pulled her phone out. "Well, we can call Leilani and get to the bottom of this right now," she said.

"Why the fuck you gotta bring Leilani into this?" I yelled. Honestly, I didn't want her to call because I knew that she was telling the truth. Niggas lied, but that didn't mean I would stop fucking Sin just because he had a girl. It surely didn't stop me from giving him some ass to begin with.

I told myself last night that I wouldn't fuck him again. But deep down inside, I knew I was giving him some of this good boy pussy just as soon as I had an opening to. That dick was too good to resist! Fuck Sky, fuck Leilani, and fuck what anybody else had to say about it.

"Sis, you awfully invested in this nigga," Sky noted. "A nigga you hardly even know at that."

"Bitch, what is up with this beef you got with Sin? Do *you* want the nigga?" I challenged.

"Of course not! But if I wanted his ass, I could've had him like that," she bragged, snapping her fingers. "That nigga's for everybody. He belongs to the streets."

"Well, that's something you and him *clearly* have in common."

"Excuse me?!" Sky spat, rolling her neck. "What the fuck does that mean?"

"It means you a hoe! Bitch, look at you!" I hollered at you. "Pregnant by your side nigga, living with your baby daddy, fucking your former boss—"

"Bitch, I never fucked Tommie!"

"Your hoe ass could've fooled me!"

"Bitch, you big mad! Don't shoot the messenger. I'm only stating facts! That nigga Sintana ain't shit! He even followed me from work and tried to rob me one night!"

I shook my head at Sky. I just knew she was lying to further convince me to leave Sintana alone. "Yeah, right."

"Why would I lie?!"

"Bitch, Sintana got his own bread! Plus, he be with all the rappers and industry niggas," I told her. "You really expect me to believe he would rob your dusty ass, of all people? Bitch, you'll say anything."

"I'm telling you the truth!" she argued. "Why do you think I told him we didn't want any trouble the day that he approached you?"

"That's simple," I shrugged. "'Cuz you wanna fuck him."

Sky's mouth dropped in shock.

"You wanna see if that dick is just as good as Leilani said it is," I smiled. "And let me tell you, sis. It is."

"You fucked him?!" Sky yelled, causing a few patrons to look our way.

"Multiple times," I boasted. "I let that nigga cum in my ass till the sun set."

Sky looked mortified. Then, she picked up an olive and

threw it at me from across the table. "Bitch, what part of Sin is Leilani's man don't you understand? How you gon' fuck my cousin's nigga?!" It was obvious who's side she was on and that pissed me off.

I grabbed an olive and threw it back at her. "And what part of I don't give a fuck don't you understand?"

"Bitch, you's a homewrecking ass hoe!" Sky shouted.

"I ain't a home wrecker if he opened the door. He let the hoe in!" I argued. "Get your facts straight, bitch!"

Suddenly, Sky snapped and launched the entire cup of olives at my head. "Bitch, fuck you!"

I threw my cup of Sangria in her face, splashing the wine all over her maxi dress. "Fuck you too! Get out yo feelings, hoe! Don't nobody care about your ugly, flat, saggy-chested ass cousin! Titties looking like empty IV bags!"

"At least her shit is real! Miss Build-a-Body!!!"

"At least I can afford surgery! I'm sure if you could, you'd be first in line to get them big ass ears clipped down! DUMBO!!!"

"FUCK YOU, HOE!!!"

"FUCK YOU TOO, BUM ASS BITCH!!!"

Sky surprised me when she launched her fist at my face and connected with my nose. In all the years we'd been friends, she had never put her hands on me. I guess everyone had their breaking point, but so did I.

Grabbing her by the hair, I punched her in the face as hard as I could drawing blood. I didn't give a fuck if she was pregnant. Her mouth certainly wasn't.

People quickly rushed over and pulled us apart before we killed each other. My nose was leaking and her mouth was busted but this shit was a long time coming.

"BITCH, I'M THROUGH WITH YOUR TRIFLIN' ASS!!!" Sky yelled, kicking and screaming. "I don't have time for fake friends! Either be real or be gone!"

"Oh, trust me, I been over you, hoe!" I shot back. "And tell your niggas to stay outta my DMs! Them niggas be obsessing over a bitch! All on my IG stories! Haven, Blade, all of 'em!" I bragged.

"The only nigga obsessed with you is that ugly ass, diseased-infested whore of a man you got! You and that nigga need to get ya'll loose assholes swabbed so that you can take several seats, bitch!!!"

Hearing her say that ignorant shit made me spit right in her fucking face as she was restrained. The bitch was disgusting and disgraceful, and I couldn't believe that I actually thought she was a friend.

"I am so sick of your ignorant, dusty, hypocritical ass!" I shouted at her.

"Bitch, I *been* sick of you!" she countered.

"YOU KNOW WHAT, BITCH? I HOPE THEM NIGGAS FINISH YOU OFF!" I hollered as I wished death on her. "I DOUBT THEY'LL MISS THE NEXT TIME!!!"

I watched the fire leave her eyes as I was escorted from the restaurant by the manager. After today, I knew we'd never go back to being friends. That ship had long since sailed.

21

SKY

After the heated altercation with Zuri, I went back home to calm down since I had some time to kill before Chosen got out of school. I was still mad as fuck and I couldn't believe she had the audacity to come for me. If the shoe was on the other foot, and I was fucking with a grimey ass nigga that wasn't shit, I would've wanted her to set me straight.

What type of friend would I be if I let her do some shit that could potentially get her caught up? And if Leilani had fucked Flex, I would have gladly put her in her place as well. I wasn't the type of bitch to stand by and let those I cared about be done dirty. I had too much dignity about myself, while these hoes lacked all virtues. Who the fuck raised these bitches? These hoes had no morals.

And Sin was flat out disgusting. How the fuck was he going to be in a relationship with my cousin and fuck my best friend behind her back, who just so happened to be trans? Leilani was going to flip once she found out!

Sintana wanted his cake and his fork to eat it. And what he didn't realize was that every secret eventually came to light, and soon his secrets would be spilling out of his proverbial closet.

I had just pulled into the designated parking space in front of my apartment building when I spotted Haven standing in front of my door with his arms crossed. He looked unhappy about having to wait for me, but no one told his dumbass to leave his keys. No one also told him to bring his goofy ass back home. When I told his ass I wanted him out of my life, I meant that shit.

Turning off my engine, I climbed out of the car and slowly approached him. I was almost tempted to go upside his head. I was still mad at his ass for pulling a gun on me. Especially with everything that me and my son had just been through. How dare he force us to relive that horror!

I also had to give the police a statement since they came right after he and Rebel left last night. I was quickly becoming a nuisance to my neighbors. It seemed like every other week there was drama, a robbery, or shootout of some sort, and I always had something to do with it. It was like I was a bad omen or some shit.

"I thought I told you not to bring your black ass back here," I said once I reached him. "You've been permanently benched."

Both of his eyes were still black and there was a small cut on his bottom lip. He'd gotten his ass handed to him yesterday. So much for protecting us. How could he protect us when he couldn't even protect himself?

"Where the fuck else was I gon' go?!" he asked.

"Honestly, I don't give a fuck where you go. I'm done taking care of a grown ass man—especially a grown ass man that still acts like a little ass kid."

"How the fuck do you expect me to act when I leave the crib and two minutes later you in bed with some fuck nigga?! How the fuck else am I supposed to deal with that shit?! The shit was foul as fuck! I had every right to go ape shit!"

"You had no fucking right to shoot up my place though! I could've gone to jail behind that shit, Haven!" His ass didn't seem to comprehend that shit. "What if Chosen had gotten hurt?"

Unbeknownst to him, the police had found my unregistered pistol and confiscated it. They could've charged me and hauled my ass off to jail, but instead they gave me a fair warning. God was in my favor that night—no thanks to those two knuckleheads.

If I didn't draw a line between us soon, they would eventually be my undoing. I couldn't afford to let their asses drag me down so I had to cut them both off. It was the only logical thing I could think to do. Plus, I felt like I was better off without them. Those two had been nothing but trouble since the day I got with them.

"Man, fuck allat. I had every right to turn up. You had me fucked up! And best believe I'mma find that nigga and open his chest up. I owe that nigga a clip for swervin' in my lane."

"Why you ain't keep this same energy with Sin? Huh? That nigga tried to rob me and slapped the shit out of my ass, and you ain't do a fuck ass thing about it!" I yelled at him.

"What?!" he growled. "You never told me that shit! Why you wait till now? Is you fuckin' with me, 'cuz if not I'll go see 'bout that nigga right now. On the dead homies, I'll give dat bitch ass nigga da business!!!"

"How about you go see about the niggas that shot at us? Since you got so muthafuckin' much energy! Go see about them niggas! You want to act hostile with somebody? Act hostile with them! And hopefully, you won't get yo ass beat like you did yesterday."

Haven sucked his teeth. "Bitch, ain't nobody get they ass beat," he said in denial, like I wasn't in the room and saw with my own two eyes. He'd gotten his ass dog-walked, plain and simple. I had to pull a gun on Rebel just to get the nigga off of him. If I hadn't intervened when I did, he would've killed Haven.

"I guess I need my eyes checked then, huh?"

"Bitch, whatever, open the fucking door. It's colder than a whore's heart out here," he complained. "I'm tired of standing."

He was right. The weather was disrespectful, but I could care less about him freezing his ass off. "Oh, it's cold, huh? Well, you know where it's warm? At your parents' crib in San Diego," I told him with a no-nonsense expression.

"Damn, so you really just gon' put a nigga out? If the shoe was on the other foot and I did that shit to you, you would've been trying to take my head off too. Ya'll bitches love to talk about equality and shit, but when ya'll do some shit, ya'll expect us to look the other fuckin' way. That don't reflect an age of equality."

"Nigga, I don't know 'bout none of that. But if you don't get your equal opportunity having ass off my doorstep, you gon' have a fucking problem," I warned him.

Haven sucked his teeth and walked off. "Don't think for a second any nigga will ever match up to me," he tossed over his shoulder.

I simply shook my head at him. "Are you going to your parents' place?" I called after him. "Just so I know what to tell our son."

"Fuck nah! I'm going to see that nigga Sin. And once I finish with his ass, I'm delivering smoke to that nigga, Rebel. I owe that nigga a hollow point to the heart, and I ain't sleepin' till I put that nigga in the dirt!"

I watched him leave and let myself into my home. *Good riddance*, I thought. I was fed up with all men. All these niggas weren't about shit. And as far as Rebel went, I was sure that he could handle himself. But Sin... I would've paid good money to see him get his ass beat.

Speaking of ass whoopings, Zuri was lucky she got dragged

away when she did. Because even this baby wouldn't have been enough to stop me from fucking her ass up. I should've been kicked my foot off in her ass when she ratted me out to Tommie. But I gave her ass the benefit of the doubt because we were friends. But I was starting to feel like she was just a wolf in sheepskin all along.

Was she ever a real friend to me? Or had she always been hating on me, on the low? My mom would always say 'don't fear the enemy that attacks you, but the fake friend that hugs you'.

22

HAVEN

After making some calls and working my moves, I was able to track down Sin. I found his scheming ass at Club Allure, popping bottles in VIP like he hadn't tried to rob my baby mama a few months back. If Sky had told me that shit sooner, I would've been dealt with the nigga accordingly. I didn't understand why she chose to sit on that information and then air it out when it was convenient for her. But that was bitches for you.

Petty as fuck.

Mobbing my way through the crowd, I made my way over to his VIP section. Sin was so busy having the time of his life, he didn't even notice me walking toward him. A thick, dark-skinned bottle girl walked past, carrying a wine bucket and I snatched the bottle out of its bucket.

"Hey!" she called out to me. "What the hell are you doing?! You gotta pay for that!"

Ignoring her, I quickened my pace toward Sin. His capped-out ass was laughing it up when I smashed the bottle over his head, shattering it on impact.

A few nearby women screamed and backed up in surprise. No one saw that shit coming including Sin.

His body dropped to the floor in a heap, his arm twisted behind his back at an awkward angle. He was unconscious before he even hit the surface. Dark red blood trickled down his face and created a puddle around his head. I didn't give a fuck and I still kicked him in his shit, knocking out two of his teeth.

Leaning down, I grabbed him by his hair and forced him to look up at me. Sadly, he was still unconscious, so he didn't hear a word that I said but I still spoke to him as if he were listening.

"Pussy nigga, you tried to rob my bitch? You was supposed to be my boy!" I kicked him in his face again, dislocating his nose. Blood sprayed onto my Nike sneakers, turning them from white to red.

I got a few more kicks in, then security came and grabbed me up. His boys didn't even bother stepping in, which let me know they were pussy too.

"Come on, bro, you gotta go," a security guard said as he seized my arm and dragged me toward the exit.

"Fuck off me, nigga!" I yelled, snatching away from him.

Running back over to Sin, I kicked him in the side of his stomach, not giving a fuck that he was still out cold. His face was a crimson mess and his arm looked like it was dislocated. I had beaten him within an inch of his life. I wouldn't stand for any man harming the mother of my child.

Sin groaned in pain, slowly coming to, and I climbed on top of him and started punching his ass repeatedly. His skull bounced off the floor with every strike. On my granny, I was determined to kill this nigga.

Sky might've been a hoe. She might've gotten knocked up by some other nigga in the streets. She might've even dragged my name through the mud. But she was still the mother of my son and my future wife, and I'd be damned if I let anyone hurt her and get away with it.

Two security guards rushed over to pull me off of Sin before I murdered his ass and I managed to spit on him before they carried me away. "Fuck nigga! You's a dead nigga!" I threatened.

Security threw me out of the nightclub and demanded I leave before they called the cops on me. I didn't give a fuck. I had smoke for anybody that wanted it! Badge or no badge!

I shoved one of the security guards back in retaliation and he punched the shit out of my ass, sending me crashing to the floor.

"You'd better get the fuck on 'fore shit get crazy!" he warned me.

I wanted to go in his mouth for putting his hands on me, but my beef was with Sin, not him. Besides, making problems for myself had never been something I was particularly fond of.

Picking myself up off the ground, I stalked toward my car with a homicidal look in my eyes. Now that I'd dealt with Sin, it was time for me to handle that bitch ass nigga Rebel. We still had some unfinished business... And I still had a bullet with Blade's name on it too.

23

BLADE

Me and Smurf were in Jessica's kitchen, breaking down the brick and packaging it to be sold when I noticed him cut his finger by accident on the razor blade. Smurf had to teach me how to do it 'cuz a nigga was not 'bout this life. Don't get me wrong, I was a hustler in every sense of the word, but a nigga had never sold a drug a day in his life. It just wasn't my lane. Haven, however, seemed made for it.

Speaking of Haven, I hadn't seen or heard from him since he'd been discharged from the hospital. I still couldn't believe I didn't kill that pussy nigga when I had the chance. Luck was on his side that day.

Fortunately, I had a lil' bit a luck of my own in the form of an Armenian mafia. Tommie had kept his word and made sure that nothing happened to me or my family. He'd even employed a few men to stay by my side and sit outside my crib to ensure my safety. If a nigga wanted to get at me, they would have to get past them first.

Anyway, I noticed as we were chopping up the work that Smurf had cut his fingers on the razor blade several times. We weren't wearing any gloves and the drugs were all in our cuticles. Instead of stopping to put a bandage on his shit or slowing down, Smurf just sucked his finger dry and went back to cutting up the coke.

"Bruh, you gone fuck around and get high as fuck, you keep doing that shit," I warned him.

"Ah, man, I'mma be a'ight," he waved me off. "You just worry 'bout all this bread we finna make," he said with an arrogant smile.

I felt like a man now that I'd bought my first bird and I couldn't wait to sell it off and gain Tommie's trust. Maybe I could even work my way up the ranks and become his lieutenant someday. A nigga wasn't trying to hug the block forever. I wanted to get the fuck up out of LA—maybe move the fam to San Fran. I'd always heard the Bay was nice.

"Blade, what the fuck?!" I heard Jessica scream from the top of her lungs. "Blade, get in here!" she hollered.

Smurf looked up at me and smirked. His ass was single so he never had to go through the shit I went through on a daily basis.

"Damn, bae, I'm in here doin' somethin'!" I yelled back. Whatever she wanted to show me could wait.

"I don't give a fuck, nigga! I told you to get your black ass in here!" she barked.

Or maybe it couldn't wait.

"Yo, who da fuck is you talkin' to like that?!" I spat.

Smurf cut his fingers again by mistake and sucked the blood off like a fucking vampire. We'd been chopping this shit up since morning and I had only cut myself once. Why the fuck was this nigga so damn clumsy? If I didn't know any better, I'd think he was doing the shit on purpose, just to have a reason to sample the goods.

"BLADE!!!!" Jessica yelled like she was possessed.

"Damn, here I come!!!" I bit back. I, begrudgingly, stood from my seat and left the kitchen.

"GET YOUR ASS IN HERE!!!" Jessica demanded.

"Aye, I'll be right back," I tossed over my shoulder. "Don't slice your fucking hand off while I'm gone," I teased Smurf, not knowing how severe his drug addiction truly was.

Dusting my hands off on my jeans, I made my way to AJ's room, where Jessica stood with an attitude. She had one hand perched on her hip and the other holding my loaded gun.

"Why the fuck do you just be leaving this shit around?!" She hounded me. "I found AJ playing with it! He had the fucking barrel in his mouth, nigga!!!"

I calmly took the gun from her and tucked it in my waistband.

Jessica hauled off and punched me in the chest. "What if he had squeezed the fucking trigger, nigga?! What if our son had killed himself?!" she cried.

Suddenly, I remembered Sky having the same fear and I assured Jessica that she had nothing to worry about. I didn't realize until now how dangerous it was having a gun around my kid. And I failed to remember that AJ could walk on his own now, though barely.

"My bad, bae. From here on out, I'mma keep the shit put up," I promised her.

"My bad??? Nigga, that's all you got to say is my bad???"

"Fuck else you want me to say? I made a mistake! From here on out, I'mma do better, damn. If you would keep an eye on the muthafucka, you wouldn't have to worry 'bout him putting a gun in his mouth!"

Jessica slapped me so hard I saw stars. "Nigga, I am so sick of dealing with your stupid ass!"

I grabbed her hard as fuck by her throat and slammed her against the wall. "If you ever put ya fuckin' hands on me again, you won't have to worry 'bout dealing with me 'cuz yo ass gon' be a dead bitch!" I let her go and she started gasping for air.

I walked past AJ, ignoring the incredulous look on his face.

Making my way back to the kitchen, I noticed that it was unusually quiet on Smurf's end. I didn't hear him chopping up the drugs like he was just a second ago.

"The fuck?"

I walked into the kitchen and immediately I knew something was wrong. Smurf was gone, along with the brick I had just purchased from Tommie. He'd even taken the loose powder on the table.

"Fuck no!" I snatched out my gun and ran to the front door. "Fuck no! Fuck no! FUCK NO!!!" I yelled, snatching the door open.

Smurf was nowhere in sight. His crackhead ass had taken off with my drugs, leaving me with a shit load of debt that I would have to pay to the Kasabian Cartel somehow!

"That snake ass nigga!!!" I yelled at the sky. "I'mma kill his muthafuckin' ass!!!"

That karma hit different when you were on the receiving end.

24

REBEL

S ky had been avoiding my ass like a bill collector, despite
me blowing her shit up repeatedly—and I couldn't say I
blamed her. I had treated her worse than an enemy and
she was supposed to be my best friend. I wouldn't have been
surprised if she cut me off permanently this time. It wasn't like I
didn't deserve it.

Back when we first started fucking with each other, I told
myself that I would always put her on a pedestal and treat her
like a queen. But ever since I lost my father, I'd been doing the
complete opposite. If I didn't get my shit together, I'd probably
lose her to someone else, and I couldn't bear the thought of
that happening.

I'd be crushed if she ended up with some other nigga, and
had my kid calling him dad. This was my first baby and I
wanted desperately to be a part of its life. I had always wanted a
shorty and now Sky was robbing me of the privilege of being a
father. But I knew I had brought this shit upon myself.

I should've never played mind games with her. I should've
never made promises that I couldn't keep. I should've never put

her second. And I shouldn't have stayed away for sixteen long years. What the fuck was I thinking? Now I would have to do everything in my power to gain her trust back and that was no easy feat.

I promised myself that if she gave me another shot, I wouldn't fuck it up. I told myself that I would do everything in my power to keep her happy and keep our family together, because I couldn't let some other nigga claim what was destined to be mine all along. Sky was put on this earth for me and not even a gun to my head could convince me otherwise.

I wanted to be with her more than I wanted anything in life, but I knew that I had to tie up a few loose ends first. So, later on that day, I took a drive up to Yobo Spa with my assault rifle and attached scope and my Glock 17.

Thomas Sr. had made a special appearance that day. I called it a special appearance because the nigga usually flew under the radar. He was a hard man to catch up with and I had been combing the streets of Cali faithfully ever since my release from the hospital. I had yet to bump into Tommie, but his dad was a lil' easier to find, so I figured I'd deal with his ass first.

After that talk in the sauna, I knew that Tommie's dad was responsible for the murder of Sky's parents. She might not have a vengeful bone in her body, but I was no stranger to being vindictive. I owed it to her and to myself to clap back at that nigga for what he did.

Screwing a suppressor on my assault rifle, I parked across the street from the spa and pulled a black ski mask over my face. I didn't want his employees to recognize me. If they saw me coming a mile away, they would give him a heads up and I couldn't have that.

Tucking my Glock in the waistband of my jeans, I climbed out of my car and crept stealthily across the street. It was night time so I wasn't easy to spot, especially since I was wearing all black.

Making my way toward the entrance, I tightened my grip on the rifle and calmly opened the door. An Asian female receptionist looked up and smiled, assuming I was a regular.

She did an automatic double-take when she saw the ski mask and the gun in my hand. She opened her mouth to scream and I pointed my rifle at her head, then lifted my finger towards my mouth and signaled for her to remain silent.

She obediently did as she was told and I quietly walked over to her and demanded she tell me where Thomas Sr. was.

Panicking, she started speaking in Korean, too spooked to realize I didn't understand her.

"English, bitch!" I growled.

"The back! He's in the back!" she said, pointing toward the rear of the spa.

"Where in the back?!" I asked her through clenched teeth.

"The steam-room! Room two!" she said, cowering in fear.

"Get the fuck out of here," I told her before making my way to the back of the spa. I didn't want her anywhere in the vicinity when shots started flying. I wasn't in the business of taking innocent lives.

I didn't have to ask twice as she made a beeline toward the exit door.

As soon as I reached the steam room, I noticed that Thomas Sr. had two of his guards stationed out front, keeping watch. The minute they saw me, they reached for their weapons—but I was much quicker on the draw.

I lit their asses up with my assault rifle, keeping the noise to a minimum with the suppressor. Thomas Sr. obviously didn't hear the ruckus, seeing as how he didn't come out to investigate.

I quickly changed my magazine and opened the door to the

steam room. I wasn't at all surprised to find him getting his dick sucked by one of his Korean employees. The young girl barely looked of age and since Thomas Sr. was a procurer of prostitutes, I assumed she was an underage immigrant.

"What the fuck?!" Thomas Sr. took one look at me and shoved the girl out of his lap. He made a move to grab his gun, but one shot to the shoulder halted him in his tracks.

The underage prostitute screamed and ran out of the room.

"*Aarrgghhh*!" he cried in pain. "What the fuck?! What the fuck is this shit about? What do you want? Money? 'Cuz if so, I can get you money. Trust me though, you don't wanna do this!"

"As a matter of fact, I do..."

Thomas Sr. was so distracted by his pain, he didn't recognize my voice. "This is a fucking suicide mission! If you kill me, everybody in LA will be on your ass! You can believe that," he said, bargaining for his life.

"I'll take my chances," I said before putting a slug in his head.

AFTER LEAVING Tommie's dad slumped in a sauna, I went back to my place, showered, stashed my guns, and made my mother something to eat. Denver still wasn't in the best of moods but she had started reading the Bible I'd given her, and for that I was grateful. She had to understand that if you didn't heal what hurt you, you would bleed on people who didn't cut you.

Over time, we would get back to how things were. But all we could do now was take baby steps.

Anyway, after making sure my stepmom was good, I drove to Sky's apartment in Glendale. I didn't call when I arrived, and since her car was in the driveway, I knew that she was home.

Parking my car next to hers, I got out and knocked on her

door. Moments later, she answered, wearing nothing but a skimpy little robe. Her face, however, didn't look anywhere near as welcoming as her body did. She was obviously upset that I was there.

"Since folks know I'm unemployed now, they think they can just pop up at my place whenever they want," she said sarcastically.

"That's why I'm here," I told her. "A nigga just wanna make sure you good."

Sky didn't even try to let me inside her home.

"I'm okay," she said honestly.

"Well, just in case..." I gave her an envelope with $20,000 inside, along with Thomas Sr.'s jewelry. She could pawn it if she needed to.

"What's this?" Sky asked confused.

"Just a lil' somethin' to hold you over..." I took a deep breath and ran a hand over my locs. I desperately needed a retwist. "And about that shit you found on me... I flushed it all," I told her.

"Really?"

"On my pops, that shit is gone," I promised. I'd gotten rid of it the day she confronted me about the drugs. I couldn't be strung out *and* be somebody's father. I had to pick one or the other. Plus, I saw how much it had hurt Sky. I didn't wanna keep hurting her.

"Good," she said. "You don't need it."

She was right; all I needed was her.

"Listen... I'mma make a couple moves and then...once I have everything squared away... I want you and Chosen to move to Malibu with me." As a kid, it was always my dream to move her out to Malibu.

Sky raised an eyebrow in surprise.

"I promised you that house off the coast. And I'mma see to

it that we turn that dream into reality," I told her with an earnest smile.

I felt like I existed when she was with me and that I didn't when she was not. Living without her was torture. I needed her in my life.

"I don't care how hard being together is, Sky... nothing is worse than being apart."

25

TOMMIE

I was playing a couple rounds of golf at *Mile Square Golf Course* in Fountain Valley when I got a call from Darius, my second-in-command. "What's up, D, can it wait? I'm in the middle of somethin' here," I told him.

Golf was my escape—my therapy without the meds or the endless ramblings of a counselor.

"Nah, Boss Man." He spoke in a somber tone. "This shit can't wait..."

"What is it?"

"It's..." He paused and released a deep sigh. "It's your pops, man."

"What happened?" I asked him. "Did the old man finally croak?" I chuckled.

There was a long silence on Darius's end. "Somethin' like that."

My grip on the phone tightened. "What? That was a joke," I told him.

"I'm sorry but this is no laughing matter, Sir..."

"So, what you're telling me is my father's dead...?" I asked for verification. I was still somewhat in denial.

"My men just found him this morning. He and a couple of his guys were murdered at Yobo Spa after hours. The receptionist claimed to have come in contact with a masked man before he was killed."

"Is she with you right now?!" I spat.

"Yes."

"Don't let that bitch out of your sight! I wanna hear every little detail about what happened," I explained. "I'm on my way back to the city now."

"Sir...?" Darius quickly stopped me before I hung up.

"What?!" I snapped.

"I think Rebel is responsible for this shit."

"No kidding, Einstein!" I said sarcastically before hanging up in his face.

Afterwards, I called up Flex. He'd been dragging his feet on handling business and as my enforcer, that was all bad. Now my father was dead and somebody had to pay. Don't get it twisted, though. I had never liked my old man. But just because we had our differences didn't mean I didn't care about old, bitter ass. Now he was gone and it was too late for me to tell him that shit myself.

Flex answered on the second ring. "What can I do for you, Boss Man?" he asked.

"You can find that nigga Rebel! Before I find that tranny bitch and put a bullet in her myself!" I lashed out.

Rebel had to go down for this shit. That muthafucka had to suffer!

26

ZURI

T he sun was just beginning to set when Sin called me out of the blue to see if he could come over. His voice on the phone was slightly muffled and I didn't realize why until he finally arrived.

The nigga had bruises all over his face and body, and his lips were swollen to twice their normal size.

"What the fuck happened to you?" I asked as I let him in my place.

Flex was out running the streets and doing whatever he had to as Tommie's little bitch, so I figured it wouldn't hurt to let Sin chill here for a little while. Besides, I was curious to hear what had gone down. Apparently, me and Sky weren't the only two who'd fought recently.

"Some hating ass niggas jumped me in the club," he said with a frown on his face. A face that I hardly even recognized with all the bruises and swelling.

"Oh my God, Sintana, that's awful."

"Shit, I'm used to it. Not that long ago some niggas shot at me on the E-way. I got in a bad ass car accident because of it. Nigga was all fucked up."

We both made ourselves comfortable on the living room sofa. I was re-watching the first season of Power before he popped up, but neither of us were interested in keeping up with what was happening on TV.

"Oh no! That's terrible."

"Yeah, niggas be out here hella mad," he continued.

"Oh well, fuck 'em. They'll never get ahead if they're always hating," I told him.

"That's why they mad" he said.

"Can I get you anything?" I offered. "I have some pain meds in the bathroom."

"Some ass would be nice," he smiled.

"I want to," I grinned. "But I don't know when my nigga's getting back. And what's up with you and Leilani? She ain't giving you no ass?"

"Man, I told you we just friends."

I rolled my eyes at him. "That ain't what I'm hearing."

"Fuck what you heard. I'm telling you shit ain't even like that between us." He pulled me close to him and kissed me. "I love our vibe, Z. And our sex," he added. "Shit, I'm trying to be more than just friends with you. Fuck Leilani."

I smiled and blushed, like a schoolgirl with a crush. I didn't give a flying fuck about Sky's warning. I liked Sintana and I was interested in seeing where things could go with us.

I mean, don't get me wrong. Flex had stepped up his game...but the nigga was hella late. And I knew it'd only be a matter of time before he was cheating and beating on me again. Besides, me and Leilani were cool but not that damn cool. She wasn't my BFF or no shit like that. She was just Sky's cousin. Sure, we'd hung out a few times but she wasn't someone worth being loyal to.

"But my nigga—"

"Man, fuck ya nigga," he said, kissing my neck and opening up my kimono.

Sin slowly pulled me on top of him in a straddling position and my dick stood at full attention. I used to think Flex was as good as it got but that was before I had a taste of Sin. The dick was incredible! It had quickly become addictive!

"I'm tryin' to make you my girl," he whispered as he pulled his dick out and rubbed it against mine.

"Really?" I challenged as we playfully sword-fought our penises.

"Yeah... Nobody gotta know," he said, licking my earlobe.

"I don't wanna be nobody's dirty, little secret," I told him.

"I ain't a nobody though," he teased.

We laughed and kissed each other as we continued to undress.

We were so wrapped up in one another, we didn't hear the front door open.

27

FLEX

"The fuck?!" As soon as I opened the door to my crib, I caught an eyeful of my bitch tonguing down some simp ass nigga, who didn't look like he was half the man I was.

Zuri quickly jumped out of his lap and tried to fix up her clothes. But it was too late; the damage was already done and I couldn't un-see what I had just saw.

"B—baby, it's not what you think!" she stuttered, looking and sounding just as guilty as ever.

I looked over at the nigga she was just kissing and saw the smug ass grin on his face, and all of a sudden, I just snapped!

Snatching my gun out of my waist, I emptied the clip into both of their asses. Their bodies jerked and shook as bullets ripped through their flesh. A hollow point pierced Zuri's skull and she fell backwards onto the nigga, torso riddled with bullet holes.

By the time my chamber was empty, neither one of them were moving.

Oh fuck.

Oh shit.

What the fuck did I just do?

What the fuck did I just fucking do?

My heartrate kicked into overdrive as I stood in the doorway of my home, staring at my girlfriend's lifeless corpse, strewn across a nigga I never even knew she was fucking till now.

"Baby," I croaked out, voice cracking with emotion.

I couldn't believe I had just shot Zuri. Never in my wildest dreams did I think I had it in me, even after stalling for weeks. But I guess everyone had their breaking point, and seeing her with some other nigga was certainly mine.

The crazy thing was, I'd been cheating on her for years—blatantly. I expected her to just deal with it, like my bullshit was something she was supposed to endure. But the moment I caught her slipping, I couldn't take it.

Maybe this was karma finally catching up to me, showing me what it felt like to be on the other side. And maybe that's why I snapped.

Lowering my gun, I slowly entered my house, taking in the deadly sight before me. The TV was still on, but no one was watching it. Zuri and her side nigga were stretched out on the sofa, eyes open and motionless, body filled with slugs.

I could already hear sirens in the distance. One of our friendly neighbors had called the cavalry.

"Baby," I dropped to my knees in front of Zuri and her fuck boy, and shook her knee like that would wake her up. "Baby, I'm sorry," I cried. "Baby, get up. Baby..."

I laid my head in her lap, wishing she could comfort me like she always did whenever I was stressed or having a bad day. But it was too late now. There was no going back. No righting this wrong.

"Baby, I'm sorry!" I sobbed hysterically.

After realizing the severity of what I'd just done, I turned the gun on myself, placed the barrel to my temple and pulled the trigger.

POW!

TOMMIE

THREE DAYS LATER

I was in my office at Club Allure, looking through a catalog of flower arrangements for my father's funeral that I was still in the process of planning when I heard an unexpected knock at my door. I hadn't been to my own club in ages and I wasn't sure who had decided to pop up without an invite.

"Who is it?" I growled, annoyed by the intrusion.

I was hoping it was Sky with my $450,000 she owed me. But I knew that was wishful thinking.

Darius walked inside, followed by Blade. "Someone's here to see you, Boss Man," he said as if I couldn't see that on my own.

"Can this shit wait?" I asked him in an exasperated tone. My father's death had really fucked my head up. And it was crazy because I had wanted him to kick the bucket for years. But now that he was dead, I felt like a piece of me was missing.

"Nah, man, this shit can't wait...unfortunately," Blade said with a look of disappointment on his face.

I couldn't wait to hear what he had to say.

"That is unfortunate," I agreed. "Leave us," I told Darius with a dismissive wave of my hand.

He quietly left the room, closing the door behind himself.

"Why the fuck are you in my face instead of in the streets?" I asked Blade, cutting to the chase.

"You ain't gon' believe this shit, man," he began. "But my crackhead ass homeboy just worked me over, man. The nigga got me for the whole bird, bruh. He took everything!" Blade said to my dismay.

I looked at his ass like he was crazy. "How the fuck is that my problem?!" I asked, heated.

I had a funeral to plan. I didn't have time for this bullshit or this game-goofy ass muthafucka standing in front of me right now.

"I still want my fuckin' money! Why the fuck are you tellin' me this shit, as if I'm supposed to fuckin' care?!" I yelled at him.

"You're right. It's not your problem. Matter fact, it's not a problem at all! All I need is a lil' bit more time to pay you back. I can scrape up some bread, cop a brick from someone else and sell it off."

I couldn't believe this cat. He had let some crackhead run off with my work and now he was trying to negotiate with me. I still wanted my fucking percentage—point blank period!

"You would buy a bird from someone else?" I asked him, clearly offended.

This fool was the biggest, most gullible dummy I knew. His ass was just laughably stupid. I had just told his dumb ass that I owned the city. Who else was there to cop a brick from? I had run off all the competition.

Suddenly, I felt embarrassed for agreeing to do business with Blade. The muthafucka clearly had a few loose screws. His elevator must not have went all the way to the top.

"I mean, don't get me wrong. You're a big bear, but not the only bear in the woods—if you catch my drift," he said, further insulting me.

Instead of listening to him spew more nonsense, I snatched my Glock out the top drawer of my desk and pointed it at him.

"Tommie, please! I got a son, man!" he begged, tossing his hands up in surrender. "All I need is a lil' time! I can still get you the money, man—"

POP! POP! POP! POP! POP! POP!

I filled his body with several rounds and watched him drop to the floor in a heap. Standing from my chair, I walked over to his twitching figure and let off a few more shots, until he wasn't moving anymore. "Fuck the money. And fuck you." I spat on his dead body just as Darius re-entered my office.

"You need help with something, Boss Man?" he asked, while looking at Blade's lifeless body.

"Yeah." I turned and walked back to my desk. "Help clean this shit up."

29

REBEL

That morning, I awoke with a renewed sense of determination. I felt good as fuck after lighting up that old bitch Thomas Sr. One down, one to go. The first thing I did that day was cook my stepmom breakfast, then I ordered a bouquet of roses, and had them hand-delivered to Sky's apartment. I wanted her to know I wouldn't stop pursuing her; not even if the whole Cali wanted a piece of her. She would always have my heart.

Today was also the day of Thomas Sr.'s funeral and I knew that I'd have to act fast if I wanted to finish what I had started so that I could focus all of my attention on Sky and our baby. I felt like I wouldn't be free until I freed myself of Tommie first. Part of me knew I should've done this shit a long time ago. Instead, I'd let him pawn me off on his daughter and work my fingers to the bone for him for years.

Anyway, I showered and put a suit and tie on for the occasion—even though I hadn't been invited to the service. Then, I loaded a fresh magazine into my assault rifle.

On my way to *Rosedale Cemetery*, I called up Sky to have a

little heart-to-heart with her. She, of course, answered with an attitude. "What do you want, Rebel..."

"You know what I want," I told her. "You..."

"You don't believe in giving people space, do you?" she asked.

I smiled. "I've given you more than enough space, my heart," I said. "Holding on to anger is like holding onto an anchor and jumping into the sea. If you don't let it go, you'll drown, baby."

Sky was silent, and I almost thought she hung up on my ass till I looked at my phone and saw that the time was still going.

"Did you get my roses?" I asked her.

"Yes, Rebel, I got them."

"How's Chosen?"

"He's fine. He's playing his game as usual."

"How's my baby?" I asked next.

I could hear her smiling through the phone. "He's fine too."

"He? How do you know it's a he?"

"I don't know. And I won't for another three months. But I guess you can say I have a feeling it's a boy."

"Well, I have a feeling it's a girl."

"Well, put some money on it, nigga," she teased.

We laughed, and in that moment, it felt like old times. It didn't feel like I was on my way to kill someone.

"I love you, Sky. And I can't wait to see you. I can't wait for us to be a family."

"I love you too, Rebel..."

"Will you choose me always?" I asked her.

She paused and mulled over the question. "Of course, will you choose me?"

"Again, and again," I told her. "See you soon."

After hanging up from Sky, I pulled across the street from the cemetery and found the perfect vantage point. Pulling out my assault rifle, I screwed the scope onto it and peered through the lens.

Thomas Sr.'s casket had just been lowered into the ground and Tommie was in the middle of it all, giving some bullshit ass heartfelt speech—as if he didn't hate the old nigga's guts. He was probably more happy than me that his old man was dead.

As I watched him recite whatever bogus sermon he was giving, I thought about our final moments together and how he'd murdered my father in cold blood.

How he'd handed Flex his gun to finish me off. "Handle this shit for me. I'm done wasting time on this asshole," he had said, like I was nothing more than a dubious task.

"With pleasure," Flex smiled before putting six rounds in me.

My eyes shot open after I heard the echoes of gunshots from that night, and I studied Tommie through the lens. It looked like he was wrapping up his little farewell speech. Little did he know, he was going in the ground with his old man.

"Adios, old friend..." I said to myself.

POW!

I squeezed the trigger, and a lone bullet soared through the Earth's atmosphere before piercing Tommie's skull, killing him instantly. He doubled over from the impact, his body collapsing into the very hole that held his father's casket. The poetic justice wasn't lost on me, but there wasn't time to savor it.

From where I sat, parked in my car, I could hear the screams erupting as chaos unfolded. People scrambled, voices rising in panic and disbelief. I stayed rooted for a moment, watching it all play out through the rearview mirror—the frantic movement, the confusion, the wails of mourning morphing into fear.

But I couldn't linger. This wasn't a victory to celebrate, not here, not now. With one last glance at the chaos I'd unleashed, I shifted into drive and peeled off, the tires screeching against the asphalt. My heart pounded, adrenaline still coursing through me as the reality of what I'd done sank in.

Tommie Kasabian was dead. The man who murdered my father, who put my stepmom in a wheelchair, was finally gone.

And yet, as the road stretched out before me, I couldn't shake the feeling that this wasn't the clean slate I thought it would be. Revenge always came with a price, and I couldn't help but wonder what mine would be.

30

SKY

A s promised, Rebel stopped by to see me later on that day, and he brought take-out, which was ridiculous since I'd already cooked for him. I'd tried my best to make his favorite meal; four cheese truffle mushroom lasagna —but it wasn't anywhere near as good as the dish his personal chef prepared for him on a weekly basis. Rebel still ate every bit of it, while Chosen helped himself to the Chinese food.

Speaking of Chosen, he was elated to have Rebel back in his life. After they finished dinner, he insisted on showing Rebel how to play Fortnite on his PS5. When his bedtime rolled around, I bathed him and tucked him in, and me and Rebel said our prayers with him.

I was shocked that Rebel went out of his way to do that, since he claimed to have been brought up in an atheist house-hold. But I was happy, nonetheless. Being with him felt so right and I knew I'd made the right decision by choosing him instead of Haven. Sure, Haven was my baby daddy, but he had a lot of growing up to do and I couldn't wait around while he slowly matured.

Rebel was grounded in life. He took care of his family, by any means necessary, my son adored him, and I knew he would be the perfect dad. Sure, we'd had our ups and downs but we also had history. An entire childhood worth of history to be exact, and he knew me better than I knew myself. I knew that we were meant for each other from now and into the future.

Rebel knew what got under my skin. He knew how to make me smile. He knew what I expected of him, and he had no problem with living up to my expectations.

After tucking Chosen in for the night, we climbed in bed together and just cuddled. "I'm sorry for pulling a gun on you," I whispered.

Rebel pulled back and looked at me, his beautiful eyes twinkling in the darkness. Nothing needed to be said and he leaned in and kissed me passionately. I kissed him back as he held me in his arms, afraid to let go as if the world would try to tear us apart.

Neither of us could pull away as our need for each other swelled and we kissed in desperation and longing, our tongues intertwining and dancing around each other as if on their own accord.

After what felt like an eternity, we broke our embrace and held each other closely, breathless in our passion. Rebel gazed into my eyes, like he wanted the image of me burned into his brain.

"Thank you," he whispered.

"For what?" I asked him. At first, I assumed he was thanking me for apologizing to him.

"For not giving up on me," he smiled.

Rebel embraced me, holding me to him in a great encompassing hug that didn't crush but rather, cradled as if he was protecting me from all evil. His right hand slid up and down my back in a caressing motion and I felt like I was home after being away for too long. Without him having to say it, I knew that he would protect me at any cost. My big, gentle, dreaded, chocolate giant.

Rebel slowly undressed me, then allowed his hands to explore my torso, arms, shoulders and stomach. He ran his large hands down my back again and rested them on my firm ass. He squeezed my butt cheeks, using them to steer me towards him and kissed me.

I closed my eyes and moaned softly, tilting my head back. His hands traveled further up and he squeezed my breasts, pinching and plucking my nipples until they stood erect and proud.

"I love you, Sky," he whispered.

"*Mmm.* I never get tired of hearing that," I smiled.

Grabbing his dick, I stroked him gently in my hand. His dick was so big and girthy that I could hardly wrap my hand around it. As I softly jacked him off, he reached down and rubbed his thumb across my clit in circular motions. Then, he wet his fingers and started pinching and playing with my nipples again. The double stimulation was driving me wild!

Rebel moaned as he rubbed the swollen nub, getting me wetter and wetter with each light stroke. He was so gentle and sensual. Not at all rough and uncoordinated like Blade and Haven.

"*Oouuuh!*" I moaned.

Rebel rolled over and took his place above me in the traditional missionary position. I gazed up at him and saw the love he had for me in his eyes. He leaned down and kissed me as he pressed his dick into me gently. A few teasing inward thrusts to help me reacquaint myself with his large two-inch girth, and before I knew it, he was in.

Deeper and deeper, he sank into me, all the while staring into my eyes. I reached up and cradled his face in my hands and pulled his lips to mine. Our tongues wrestled and his thrusts became longer and more vigorous.

In a matter of seconds, you could hear what sounded like macaroni being stirred. My shit was so wet that the sheets beneath me were soaked. Rebel was fucking the shit out of my ass, and making me fall in love with him all over again.

Until now, I hadn't realized that I'd never made love before.

Longer and deeper, stronger and faster, he hammered into me while holding my intense gaze. I raised my hips to meet his every thrust, wishing it could last for an eternity. Fucking him felt so good.

Rebel grunted as he struggled to keep a steady pace, but it was getting harder and harder for him the wetter I got.

"Shit, Sky. This pussy is somethin' else," he moaned.

I wrapped my legs around him and pulled harder on him. His thrusts became more powerful, and I clamped down on his hard dick to keep him right where I wanted him. In between my thighs forever.

My mouth hung open and my eyes rolled to the back of head as I felt myself reaching my peak. My legs shuddered around him as he continued to fuck me unmercifully, ramming my G-spot repeatedly. My pussy muscles contracted and I suddenly gushed all over his big, black dick.

Rebel pulled out his slick meat and climbed down at my waist to lick up all the cum. He sucked my clit a little and probed my opening with the tip of his tongue, then climbed back up to stick it in.

"*Oouuuh*," I whimpered.

In that moment, nothing else existed except Rebel making me cum.

Suddenly, I felt his dick twitch inside me and he gave one last, powerful thrust as I screamed from my second orgasm. His hot seed gushed into me and I could feel his cum flowing into my body. I clamped my legs tighter around him as he emptied everything he had into me. I never wanted to let go as we came together in ecstasy.

"I love you, Rebel. I love you so much."

He slowly lowered himself onto his elbows, his dick still buried in me, to avoid crushing me. I was happy that he didn't pull out just yet because I enjoyed the skinship. "Remember when we first met?" he suddenly asked.

EPILOGUE
ONE YEAR LATER

Rebel had kept his promise and moved us into a beautiful, state-of-the-art mansion in Malibu, near the beach. As a matter of fact, it was within walking distance and I couldn't have been more overjoyed at the highly-desirable location.

Chosen loved living by the water and he had made so many friends at his new school. A few of them had even taught him how to surf in exchange for him teaching them sign language—though I didn't let him venture too far out on his own.

We ended up moving Denver into our new home so that we could properly care for her. She didn't like me when we first met, but after a while, she warmed up to me. She didn't really have a choice, seeing as how I'd married her stepson.

Our wedding was small and intimate, just like we wanted it. A quiet ceremony under a canopy of twinkling lights in the backyard of Rebel's childhood home. It wasn't extravagant or flashy—just close friends and family, the people who had stood by us through thick and thin. I wore a simple white dress, and Rebel looked devastatingly handsome in his tailored suit, his usual ruggedness softened by the emotion in his eyes. When I walked down the aisle, hand in hand with my son, Rebel's gaze locked on me like I was the only person in the world. For the first time in my life, I felt truly seen, truly loved.

I couldn't believe I was marrying my childhood best friend. Rebel had been my rock, my protector, and my partner through so many storms. Standing there with him, promising to love him for the rest of my life, felt like coming home. He wasn't perfect—hell, neither of us were—but he was my person. The one who had always believed in me, even when I didn't believe in myself.

After we exchanged vows, I could see tears glistening in his eyes. Rebel wasn't the type of nigga to cry, but in that moment, he didn't care about holding back. And neither did I. As we kissed to seal our promises, the world around us disappeared, leaving just the two of us in that moment of pure, unfiltered love.

Despite our rocky start, Denver eventually came around. She loved her grandkids unconditionally and spoiled them every chance she got, whether it was sneaking them candy or telling them stories about their dad as a young boy. Over time, we became what I never thought I'd have—a real family. We weren't perfect, but we were happy.

Marrying Rebel didn't just give me a husband; it gave me a sense of belonging I'd been searching for my entire life. We built something beautiful out of the chaos, and every day, I thanked the universe for giving us that second chance.

Sad to say, I never got to ask Tommie how he'd met my mother because he was murdered at his father's funeral. It served his ass right and I didn't shed a single tear when I heard the news. To be honest, I celebrated his death. I had never liked him anyway. I especially hated his ass after our heated encounter in his office and I was happy that I wouldn't have to pay him back that half a mil. I never bothered to tell Rebel that he'd almost raped me. It didn't matter though because karma still ended up catching up to his old ass.

My cousin, Leilani was devastated to hear about Sin's murder, but she moved on with her life after a few months of grieving, and now she was dating a hot Brazilian guy who was currently in med school. Let her tell it, she was officially done with bad boys.

I was also crushed when I heard about what happened to Zuri. Regardless of our differences, she was my best fucking friend and the closest thing I had to a sister. I was shocked to learn that Flex had killed her and Sintana before committing suicide. I had always told her Flex would be her undoing. Too bad she couldn't get away from his ass before it was too late.

In honor of my deceased best friend, I decided to name my daughter Zuri Rose Coleman. Rebel wasn't too happy about it at first, but the name slowly grew on him. He was always letting me have my way. The man had me spoiled rotten.

Fortunately, Haven and I were able to hash things out and co-parent without any drama. He and Rebel had even squashed their beef and every other weekend they hung out at the bar together to drink and shoot pool. Life was easier when we weren't at each other's throats. I was so proud of them for putting their differences aside.

"Mommy, mommy! Look what we caught!" Chosen said, running into the house with a fish still on the hook, wriggling for dear life.

Rebel had been taking him fishing religiously, especially since we lived near the water.

"That's awesome! Now get it out of here," I laughed. It was leaking fish juices all over my beautiful marble floors.

"We're going to skin it and eat it for dinner!" Chosen insisted. His speech had improved dramatically, thanks to Rebel.

I put my hands on my hips. "Is that so?"

Before he could answer, Rebel walked into the house, carrying our daughter on his hip. Zuri Rose was perfect and she was a spitting image of her father.

"That's right. You got a problem with that, woman?" he challenged.

Denver rolled herself into the kitchen. "I do! I hate fish!" she butted in.

"Should we put it back in the water?" Chosen asked.

The fish was still squirming on the hook and it wouldn't be long until he succumbed from lack of oxygen.

"Yeah, put it back," I said, my gaze locking on Rebel. "Give him a second chance."

Sometimes, that's all anyone needed—a second chance.

THE END

Text *BOOKS* to 55444 to join our VIP list for exclusive updates, giveaways, and juicy book news!

Made in the USA
Columbia, SC
28 July 2025